AT THE GREEK
TYCOON'S
BIDDING

AT THE GREEK TYCOON'S BIDDING

BY

CATHY WILLIAMS

MILLS & BOON®

First published in Great Britain 2006
Large Print edition 2006
Harlequin Mills & Boon Limited,
Eton House, 18-24 Paradise Road,
Richmond, Surrey TW9 1SR

© Cathy Williams 2006

ISBN-13: 978 0 263 19017 5
ISBN-10:   0 263 19017 X

Set in Times Roman 16 on 19 pt.
16-1106-56009

Printed and bound in Great Britain
by Antony Rowe Ltd, Chippenham, Wiltshire

CHAPTER ONE

THEO was in the middle of reading a financial report when he heard the crash. The sound catapulted through the empty corridors of the office with ear-splitting intensity. Any other person would have reacted in shock, and probably fear. After all, it was late, and even with security guards there was no building in London that could be termed fully safe from someone determined to break and enter. Not Theo Miquel. Without bothering to arm himself with the prerequisite heavy object, dark brows knitted into an impatient frown at being interrupted, he strode out of his plush designer office, activating the switch that flooded the darkness outside with brilliant fluorescent light.

Theo Miquel was not a man to run scared of anything, least of all a would-be intruder who was clumsy enough to signal his arrival by crashing into something.

It didn't take long for him to pinpoint the origin of the interruption, for sprawled in the corridor was a trolley, the contents of which were scattered across the marble-tiled floor. Cleaning fluids, broom, mop—and a bucket of water which was slowly spreading along the tiles towards the carpeted offices on either side.

As his eyes took in the chaotic sight he heard the clamour of feet pounding up the stairs, and then the security guard was there, out of breath and bristling with apologies. They converged at the scene of the crime at roughly the same time, although it was Theo who was the first to kneel next to the inert body of the girl who had collapsed on the floor.

'So sorry, sir,' Sid stammered, watching as Theo felt for a pulse. 'I came as fast as I could—as soon as I heard the noise. I can take over from here, sir.'

'Get this stuff cleared away.'

'Of course, sir. I'm very sorry… She looked a little pale when she came in this evening, but I had no idea…'

'Stop babbling and tidy this mess up,' Theo commanded sharply.

He barely registered the flustered guard squeezing dry the mop and soaking up the spilt water before it could intrude into the expensive offices and wreak yet more havoc.

At least the girl hadn't been inconsiderate enough to die on his premises. There was a pulse, and she might be as pale as hell but she was breathing. She had fainted—probably pregnant. A symptom of the times. Controlling his irritation, he scooped her up, oblivious to the frantic worry pasted on the security guard's face. He was dimly aware that his employees, whatever their rank, treated him with a certain amount of subservience. He was unaware that this subservience teetered precariously on the brink of downright fear, so he was vastly exasperated when he glanced across to find Sid virtually wringing his hands.

'I can take care of her, sir… No need for you to get involved… Not a problem…'

'Just make sure this place is cleaned up and then you can return to duty. If I need you, I'll call.'

This was an interruption he could well have done without. It was Friday. It was after nine in the night and there was still half a report to get through if he was to e-mail the corrected copy to his counterpart on the other side of the world before their high-level meeting the following Monday.

He kicked open the door to his office and deposited the now stirring body on the long burgundy sofa which occupied one entire wall of the large room. He had not had a hand in designing the décor of his office. If he had, he would probably have chosen the barest of furnishings—after all, an office was a place to work and not a cosy sitting room in which to luxuriate—but he had found over the years, and to his surprise, that the grand, heavy opulence of the room was strangely conducive to concentration. The oak-panelled walls would have been more at home in a gentleman's club, but there was still something warm about them, filled as they were with books on finance, economics and naturally the accounts of the vast shipping empire that was the very basis of his huge inherited wealth. His desk, fashioned in a time before computers, lacked the convenient set-up to accommodate modems and fax machines and all the various appendages of twenty-first-century living, but it was pleasing to look at and did its job. The windows were floor to ceiling, and lacked the smoked glass effect of the taller, more modern offices all around, but they were charming. In the crazy rush of the city his offices, housed in a grand Victorian house, were a touch of old-world sanity.

It was more than he was currently feeling as he stared down at the girl, whose eyelids were beginning to flutter as consciousness crawled back.

She was solidly built beneath the blue and white striped overalls which covered a choice of clothing Theo would have found offensive on any woman. A thick cardigan of some indiscriminate brown colour and jeans that were frayed at the hems, their only merit being that they partially concealed heavy-duty shoes that would have been more suitable for a man working on a building site than a woman.

He waited, standing over her, arms folded, his body language informing her in no uncertain terms that, while he might have rescued her, he wasn't about to allow the act of charity to overstay its limited welcome.

And while he waited, impatience mounting, his eyes roved over her face, taking in the short, straight nose, the wide mouth, and eyebrows that were surprisingly defined and at odds with the pale curly hair that had escaped its restraints.

As her eyes fluttered open he could only assume that he had been taken by surprise, because for a few seconds a confusing surge of awareness rushed through him. She had amazing eyes. The purest and deepest of blues. Then she blinked, disoriented, and the moment was lost as reality took over. The reality of his work being interrupted when time was not on his side.

'It would appear that you fainted,' Theo informed her as she struggled into a sitting position.

Heather gazed up at the man staring down at her and felt her throat tighten. For the past six months she had worked in his offices, coming in at six-thirty when she could begin cleaning, after the bulk of the employees had left. From a distance, she had watched him out of the corner of her eye, watched as he worked behind his desk, his door flung open—although she knew, from snatches of conversation she had overheard over the months, that very few would risk popping in for a light chat. She had felt herself thrill to the tones of his dark, deep voice when he happened to talk to one of his employees. He intimidated everyone, but as far as she was concerned he was the most beautiful man she had ever laid eyes on.

The lines of his face were strong—harsh, even—but he possessed a classic beauty that was still aggressively and ruggedly masculine. Midnight-dark hair swept back from his powerful face, curling against the nape of his neck, and even though she had never had the courage to look him in the face she had glimpsed enough to know that his eyes were dark and fathomless, and fringed with lashes that most women would have given their eye teeth for. She supposed that if she had worked for him she might well have found him as forbidding as everyone else seemed to, but he had no influence over the course of her life and so she could appreciate him without fear.

Not that she was by nature the type of girl who cowered in the presence of anyone. By nature she was of a sunny disposition, and was a great believer that she was equal to everyone else, whatever her social standing might temporarily be and however broke she was. What counted lay inside and not in the outer packaging.

While her mind had been wandering down the extraordinary path that had found her lying on the sofa in his office, Theo had taken himself to his drinks cabinet and returned with a small glass of brown liquid.

'Drink some of this.'

Heather blinked and tried not to stare too hard at him. 'What is it?' she asked.

'Brandy.'

'I can't.'

'I beg your pardon?'

'I can't. It's against company policy to drink while on the job. I could get the sack and I need the money.'

As far as Theo was concerned this was far too much information. All he wanted was for her to guzzle a bit of the brandy, which would have her up and running, leaving him with sufficient time to get through what he had to do if he were to avoid an argument with the latest of his dates, whose temper had already been tested to the limit by the frequency of his cancellations.

'Drink,' he ordered, holding the glass close to her lips, and Heather nervously obeyed, taking the tiniest of sips and flushing with guilt.

'Oh, for goodness' sake!' Theo exclaimed. 'You've just fainted! One sip of brandy isn't selling your soul to the devil!'

'I've never fainted before,' Heather said. 'Mum used to tell me that I wasn't the fainting sort. Fainting was for undernourished girls, not for fatties like me. Claire fainted a lot when we were growing up. Well, not exactly *a lot,* but a few times. Which is a lot by anyone's standards…'

Theo experienced the novel sensation of being bombarded on all fronts. For a few seconds he literally lost the power of speech.

'Perhaps I'm coming down with something,' Heather remarked, frowning. She sincerely hoped not. She couldn't afford to start taking time off work because of ill health. Her night job with the cleaning company was on a temporary basis. No sick leave. And her day job as assistant teacher at a school near where she lived just wasn't sufficient for her to really make ends meet. She felt the colour drain away from her face.

Theo watched, fascinated by this transparent display of emotion, before urgently pressing the glass to her lips. The last thing he needed was another attack of the vapours.

'You need more than just a sip of this. It'll restore some of your energy.'

Heather took a bigger mouthful and felt the alcohol burn pleasantly in the pit of her stomach.

'You don't recognise me, do you?'

'Recognise you? Why on earth should I recognise you? Look,' Theo said decisively, 'I have a lot of work to get through before I leave here tonight. You can sit on the sofa till you feel rested enough to leave, but if you'll excuse me I'm going to have to return to work.' He was struck by a bright idea. 'If you like I can get that security guard chap to come and take you downstairs.'

'Sid.'

'Sorry?'

'His name's Sid. The "security guard chap". Shouldn't you know that?' Heather asked curiously. 'He's been working for you for over three years!' But, like with her, he would have seen him and not registered his face. To a man like Theo Miquel he was literally invisible.

Not liking the accusatory tone to her voice, Theo momentarily forgot the half-read financial report lying on his desk.

'It beats me why I should know the name of every security guard who's ever worked here...'

'You employ him!'

'I employ lots of people. And anyway, this is a ridiculous conversation. I have work to do and...'

'I'm an interruption. I'm sorry.' Heather sighed and felt tears well up as she contemplated the disappearance of her job should she be ill. It was the middle of January. There were a million and one viruses flying about, most of them apparently winging their way from the Far East in an attempt to find more victims.

'You're not about to cry, are you?' Theo demanded. He fished into his trouser pocket and extracted a handkerchief, cursing himself for his good nature in carrying the girl into his office. A complete stranger, no less, who now seemed intent on chatting to him as though he wasn't a very important man—a man whose valuable time was money!

'Sorry.' Heather took the handkerchief and sniffled miserably into it. She blew her nose, which made her feel light-headed all over again. 'Perhaps I'm just hungry,' she offered, thinking aloud.

Theo ran his fingers through his hair and cast

one despairing glance at the report on the desk. 'Hungry?' he said flatly.

'Doesn't that sometimes bring about fainting spells?' Heather asked, looking at him questioningly.

'I haven't quite got to that part of my nutrition course as yet,' Theo said with thick sarcasm, and she smiled. It was a smile that lit up her face. Could have lit up an entire room, for that matter. He felt inordinately pleased at having engineered this response in her. With a stifled sigh of resignation, he decided to put the report on hold for few minutes.

'I have a call to make,' he said, walking away even as he took his mobile phone from his pocket. 'I'm going to give you the land line. Use it to call for some food.'

'Oh, no! I couldn't just *order food in*!' She shuddered at the cost involved.

'You can and you will.' He looked across at her in the middle of handing her the telephone. 'If you're hungry then you have to eat something, and there's no fridge in my office with a handy supply of food. So just order whatever you like. Call the Savoy. Tell them who I am. They'll deliver whatever you want.'

'*The Savoy*?' Heather squeaked in consternation.

'On the house, Miss… Miss… I don't know your name…'

'Heather. Heather Ross.' She smiled shyly at him, marvelling at his patience and consideration, especially when you considered that from what she'd gathered, people found him scary.

Theo, she noticed, did not bother to give her his name, but perhaps he assumed that she would already know it—as indeed she did. She saw it every evening in gold plate on his door. Buoyed up by the kick from the brandy, and the realisation that hunger had brought on her unaccountable loss of strength, Heather dialled through to the Savoy, even though the practical streak in her knew that it was a ridiculous nonsense when all she probably needed was a cheese sandwich and a bottle of water. She was vaguely aware, in the background, that an urgent and hushed conversation was being conducted, one to which he clearly did not want her to be a party, and as soon as he was off the phone she turned to him with stricken eyes.

'I've messed up your arrangements for this evening, haven't I?'

She could tell that this line of conversation was not falling upon fertile ground, but her tendency to blurt out what happened to be in her head did not go hand in hand with the silent approach he clearly wanted. He would order in food for her, or rather get her to order in her own food—which she had sensibly confined to sandwiches, astounded at the effect his name had had on whoever was in charge of the reception desk at the Savoy—but beyond that he did not want her chatter.

'No matter.' He shrugged. 'I couldn't make it anyway.' Not that Claudia had seen it in quite that light. In fact, his ears were still ringing from the sound of the telephone being banged down at the other end, and he could hardly blame her. He consoled himself with the absolute fact that the minute a woman started making demands on his time it was almost certainly the time to dispose of her. In this case, the woman in question had disposed of herself.

'Was it important?' Heather asked anxiously.

'What's important is lying on my desk, waiting to be read, so if you don't mind...' He half expected her to launch into another conversation, but to his relief she maintained an obedient silence, though he couldn't stop his eyes from straying towards her every so often, distracting him from the task at hand.

By the time the food arrived—couriered over— Theo had abandoned all hope of finishing the report, at least until he had escorted her out of the building.

'Why have you not been eating?' he asked, watching as she plunged into her sandwich with the gusto of someone suddenly released from a starvation diet.

'There's no need for you to make polite conversation,' Heather said, tucking into sandwich number two. 'I know you have heaps of work to do. These sandwiches are fantastic, by the way.'

'I'll get back to work once you've gone.'

'Oh, I feel fine now. I might as well finish what I came to do.' She glanced across at him and then quickly reverted her attention back to the diminishing pile of sandwiches, just in case she found herself staring again.

'And encourage another fainting fit? I don't think that's a good idea.'

'You mean in case I cause more hassle?'

Theo didn't immediately answer. He was mesmerised by the sight of a woman eating so much. Judging by the women he knew, eating was fast becoming a dying art form. They nibbled at salad leaves or else pushed food around their plates as if one calorie too many might lead to sudden obesity.

'I'm hungry,' Heather said defensively. 'Normally I'm a very light eater, as a matter of fact. I should really be rake-thin. But I have a very stubborn metabolism. It refuses to do its job.'

'What's the name of this firm you work for? I'll call them and let them know that you're in no fit state to continue here tonight.' He reached for the telephone and was halted by her sudden squeak of panic.

'You can't do that!'

'Why not?' Black eyes narrowed shrewdly on her face. 'I take it you *are* legally registered with the company, and not involved in any moonlighting as a tax dodge…'

'Of course I'm not moonlighting!' Heather denied hotly.

'Then what's the problem?'

'The problem is that I *need* to complete this job because I *need* my time sheet to be signed downstairs! I can't afford to go home just because I felt a little sick!' Awareness of her situation rushed through her and she slung her legs over the side of the sofa. All at once, released from the temporary daze of being in his presence and no longer feeling light-headed, she realised what an unappealing sight she must make. Hair everywhere, her robust frame encased in the least flattering garment known to mankind. She hardly presented the storybook image of a fragile, appealing damsel in distress. She ran her fingers self-consciously through her hair, feeling for the elastic band that had gone a bit askew and repositioning her ponytail back to where it should be, along with all the other rebellious curls that had managed to fall out.

'Give me a minute,' she said, sucking in a few deep lungfuls of air, 'and I'll be on my way.' She stood up, and sat back down. She looked at him miserably. 'Maybe I need a few minutes,' she suggested. 'I can wait outside. I don't mind sitting on the ground—just till I gather myself. Honestly, I don't know what the matter is…'

'Are you pregnant?' Theo asked abruptly.

Heather raised horrified eyes to him. 'Pregnant? Of course I'm not pregnant! Why on earth would you think that? Oh…I know why. I'm young, I fainted, and I'm involved in manual work…therefore I must be a brainless bimbo who's stupidly managed to get herself pregnant…'

'That wasn't my reason for suggesting it…' Theo lied, discomfited by her accurate assessment of his thought processes.

'Well, then…' Another thought lodged in her head and she blushed painfully. 'It's because I'm fat, isn't it?'

Not wanting to encourage this line of conversation, and seriously concerned that getting rid of the girl might prove more difficult than he had anticipated, Theo adroitly changed the subject.

'I can't have you collapsing on my premises.' He walked over to her and looked down at the discreet name label pinned to the front of her overall. Distantly he registered that she certainly was on the plump side. Her breasts, pushing against the unyielding fabric, appeared to be voluminous. In every respect she was physically the antithesis of the women he dated, who were always leggy, brunette, flat chested and ultra-glamorous. 'Hills Cleaning Services,' he murmured to himself. 'What's the telephone number?'

Heather reluctantly provided him with the information and waited with a sinking heart as he called and explained the situation to her employer at the other end of the line.

'I've been sacked, haven't I?' she asked gloomily, the minute he was off the phone.

'Apparently there have been two incidents recently…?'

'Oh, not fainting incidents,' Heather expanded quickly, just in case he began thinking that she was one of those pathetic women who couldn't take care of themselves. 'You haven't told me what they said…'

'I thought I just had. In a roundabout way.' Unusual for him to say anything in a roundabout way, but he was reluctantly beginning to feel sorry for the woman. Overweight, insecure, and clearly ill equipped to do any other job. Thanks to him, she would now have to find alternative employment. He felt an uncustomary twinge of guilt. 'They seem to think that you're a liability…'

'That's silly,' Heather said miserably. 'I'm not a liability. I admit a couple of times I got home from work and fell asleep. I just meant to put my feet up for five minutes with a cup of tea, but you know how it is. I nodded off, and by the time I woke up it was too late to do the cleaning job...'

'You do *two* jobs...?' Theo asked in astonishment.

'I'm sorry. I know you thought you were doing the right thing, and I know you mightn't have wanted me around just in case I fainted again—which I wouldn't have, by the way—but thanks to you I'm now out of pocket. They probably won't even pay me for the hour and a half I've been here.' She stared despondently into the abyss of imminent poverty. Of course there were other night jobs. She could always do that bar one at the local pub. Tom would have her in a minute. But bar work was gruelling and exhausting. At least with the cleaning job she could switch to automatic and get through her work with her mind pleasantly drifting off to a comforting fantasy land in which she actually completed the illustration course she wanted and became famous designing the covers for children's books.

'What's the day job?' Theo asked curiously. She was now strong enough to sit up. He wasn't really interested in hearing the ins and outs of her life, but a few minutes' chat wouldn't kill him, and it would give her a bit more time to gather her resources. Her hands rested limply on her lap and she was staring into the distance, no doubt contemplating the horror of not earning minimum wages by doing a job that was draining her of all her energy. Thus far, only two women he had dated had held down jobs, and neither had actually seen their jobs as anything more than an interruption of their leisure time—something to do as an amusing distraction from the daily grind of shopping, self-pampering and lunches with their friends.

'Oh. Day job.' Heather refocused on the man looking at her and was hit by the realisation that this would probably be the last time she had the pleasure of seeing him. She felt an uncomfortable little void open up in the pit of her stomach. 'I'm an assistant teacher at the school just around the corner from me,' she said dully.

'You're an *assistant teacher*?'

His shocked tone managed to raise a smile from her. She could easily have been offended by the implied insult, but she knew that from the Olympian summits which he occupied he would simply have assumed that, as a cleaner, she would be incapable of achieving much else—just as he had assumed that her fainting fit had been brought on by pregnancy.

'I know. Incredible, isn't it?' she replied, grinning, regaining some of her lost spirit. Now she just wanted to drag the conversation out for as long as possible, bearing in mind that she wouldn't be clapping eyes on him again.

'Why do you clean offices if you have a perfectly viable daytime job?'

'Because my "perfectly viable daytime job" just about manages to pay the rent on my room and the bills and I need to save some money up so that I can afford to carry on with my studies.' Well, he might not have known her from Adam before, but he certainly appeared confounded by her revelation now—the revelation that she actually had a brain. 'You see,' she continued, enjoying his undivided attention while she had it, 'I left school quite young. At sixteen, as a matter of fact. I don't know why, but all my friends were doing that—leaving to get jobs. Not that there were a whole heap of jobs for school-leavers in the Yorkshire village I came from. But, anyway, it seemed a good idea at the time, and earning money was great. It helped out with Mum, and Claire couldn't help out there. She wanted to head to London and get into acting…'

'Claire…?'

'My sister. The skinny, beautiful one I mentioned to you?' Heather's eyes misted over with pride. 'Long blonde hair… big green eyes… She needed all the money Mum could spare so that she could get started in her career…'

This woman, Theo thought, was an open book. Had no one ever told her that the allure of the female sex lay in the ability to be mysterious? To stimulate the chase with teasing pieces of information dropped here and there? Her frankness was beyond belief. Now she was telling him all about her sister and the fabulous career that had taken her across the Atlantic, where she was now modelling and already getting bit parts in daytime soaps.

Theo held up his hand to put a stop to the deluge of personal chatter.

He hardened himself against the immediate dismay that brought a flush of pink colour to her cheeks.

'You seem to be fully recovered,' he informed her. 'I'm very sorry that you no longer have your job with the cleaning firm, but it's probably for the best if you're physically not up to it…' He stood up, decisively bringing her presence in his office to an end, and waited until she had followed suit. Her hair was still continuing to rebel against the clips and elastic band, and now she was standing up he could see that she was shorter than he had thought—at best five foot four. She smoothed down her unflattering overall and he resisted the urge to give her a piece of good advice. Namely that she would probably be able to get a decent well-paid job if she paid a bit more attention to how she looked. Employers tended to look at the general appearance of their employees and were often influenced by it, unfair though it was.

'Maybe you're right. I guess I shall just have to go and work for Tom. He won't mind if I oversleep now and again. He likes me, and he'll pay me just so long as I give him what he wants…'

Theo paused in mid-stride, holding the door open while Heather walked past him, oblivious to the horror on his face. Ever the optimist, she was already working out the pros of the job she had previously dismissed out of hand. For starters, it was close, and would involve no public transport travel—which was always a concern to her, bearing in mind what you read in the newspapers. Also, Tom would be much more lenient than the cleaning company if she accidentally skipped an evening's work. And maybe, just maybe, she could drop the name of the pub into this conversation and casually mention that Theo might like to come along and patronise it some time.

She opened her mouth to voice that tantalising suggestion, only to discover that she had been walking towards the elevator on her own. He was still standing by his door and staring at her as though she had mutated into another form of life.

'Oh!' Heather blinked, disappointed that he wasn't at least walking her to the lift, then she chastised herself for being silly. Prior to this evening the man hadn't even known of her existence, even though he must have at least glimpsed her off and on over the previous months! He had been good enough to look after her in his office, interrupting his own busy work schedule, which he had not been obliged to do. Crazy to think that he would accompany her on her journey down! She gave him a little wave. 'Thank you for being so kind and looking after me,' she said, raising her voice to cover the yawning distance between them. 'I'll just be off!'

Theo had no idea how he had managed to become unwittingly embroiled in the concerns of a perfect stranger, but, having been instrumental in getting her the sack, he felt morally obliged to question her decision about taking on a job that sounded very insalubrious indeed. Who was this Tom character? he wondered. Probably some sad old man who thought he could pay for the services of a naïve young girl in desperate need of cash. And naïve she most certainly was. Theo couldn't remember a time when he had been confronted by someone so green around the ears.

'Give me a minute.' He returned to the office, hesitated for a few seconds in front of his computer before shutting it down, grabbed his coat, his laptop and his briefcase and then exited, switching off the light behind him before closing and locking his door.

Heather was still there by the lift, looking utterly bemused. A revelation of his own senti- ments, he thought wryly. No time to fulfil his commitment to Claudia, but now perversely driven to accompany this stranger to her house because she had succeeded in rousing some kind of a sense of duty in him. He likened it to the sentiment someone might feel when confronted by a defenceless animal accidentally caught under the wheels of a car and in need of a vet.

'Are you leaving work?' Heather asked in surprise, looking up at him, wishing, for once, that she wasn't quite as short as she was. Short and stocky and stupidly thrilled just to be taking the elevator down with him. 'It's just that you don't normally leave this early.'

Theo paused to stare at her.

'You know what time I leave work in the evenings…?' He pressed the elevator button and the doors opened smoothly, as though the lift had been sitting there, just waiting for him to appear and summon it into immediate action.

Heather blushed. 'No! I mean,' she continued, dragging out the syllable, 'I just know that you usually leave after I've finished cleaning most of the directors' floor.' She laughed airily as the lift doors shut on them, locking her into a weird feeling of imposed intimacy. 'When you do something as monotonous as cleaning, you start paying attention to the silliest of details. I guess it just makes the time go past a little quicker! I know you're usually the last to leave in the evenings, along with Jimmy and a couple of others who work on the floor below.' Best change the subject, she thought. She was beginning to sound sad. 'Do you know,' she confided, 'that sandwich has done me the world of good? I feel fantastic. Do you often send out for food from the Savoy?' She sneaked a little sideways glance at him and found that he was looking at her in a very odd manner. 'Sorry. I'm chatting too much. Have you got plans for this evening?'

'Only ones that involve dropping you back to wherever it is you live…'

Heather's mouth dropped open.

'Deprived of the power of speech?' Theo said dryly. 'That must surely be a first for you.'

'You're dropping me back to my house?' Heather squeaked. Now she really *did* feel guilty. 'Please don't. There's no need.' She laid her small hand tentatively on his arm as the doors opened and they stepped outside. The contact with his forearm, even though it was through a layer of shirt, sent a burning sensation running through her and she quickly removed her hand. 'I'm not as feeble as you seem to think I am. Can't you tell from my girth that I'm a bonny lass?' She laughed self-deprecatingly but he didn't laugh back. Didn't even crack a smile.

Theo was not a man accustomed to delving into the female psyche. He had always prided himself on pretty much knowing how women operated. They expressed their interest in a certain way—the lowered eyes, the coy smile, the slight inclination of the head—and then came the game of hide and seek, a game he thoroughly enjoyed. It was only after that things took a downturn, when inevitably they began questioning the amount of time he put into his work, insinuating that he would be far better amused if he paid them more attention, because after all wasn't that what relationships were all about? They were all about trying to build a relationship with him, trying to pin him down. Insecurities never raised their heads, although in truth none of them had ever had anything much to be insecure about.

Now it occurred to him that this girl had insecurities about her weight and Lord only knew what else. Insecurities that had made her the sort of gullible woman who might be tempted by a man for all the wrong reasons.

'Your coat,' he said, 'and then I shall take you out and feed you…'

CHAPTER TWO

BECAUSE there was no convenient underground car park for the office, most of the employees who chose to drive in—willing to pay the Congestion Charge because it gave them flexibility to leave London at the drop of the hat to attend meetings elsewhere— parked at the nearest multi-storey car park.

Theo, however, had a chauffeur permanently on call. Within minutes of speaking into his mobile phone, a long, sleek Mercedes had pulled up outside the building, engine gently throbbing as it waited for them to get in.

Heather had moved on from protesting about the need to be dropped home to protesting about his invitation to dinner, which was unnecessary considering she had just eaten sandwiches courtesy of the Savoy.

She found herself ushered into the back seat of the car and slid across to make space for him.

'It's very good of you, Mr Miquel…'

'Considering you fainted on my doorstep, so to speak, I think you can call me by my first name—Theo.'

'Well, all right. But I still don't need taking anywhere. You don't have to feel responsible for me, although I'm very grateful for your help…'

Theo turned to look at her, his massive body lounging indolently against the car door.

'I can't remember the last time I was so comprehensively turned down for dinner by a woman.'

Heather squirmed, and wondered how she could temper her protests in case he thought that she was being offensive and ungrateful after all he had done for her. And she had to admit that the thought of having dinner with him was disconcerting but also exciting.

'I'm not exactly dressed for dinner,' she said, staring down at her workmanlike shoes and the thick black coat which did its job very efficiently but which also made her look a little like a ship in full sail.

'No, you're not,' Theo agreed, 'but I'm sure Henri won't mind.'

'Henri?' So he agreed she looked a complete

mess. Well, her success rate with the opposite sex had never been that sparkling. At least not when it came to the sexual side of things. She had grown up in the shadow of her beautiful sister and from an early age had resigned herself to the inevitability of always taking second place. Boys had been her best mates, but they had been enthralled by Claire. That was simply life, and she had never let it get her down.

Right now it *was* getting her down.

'The proprietor at a little French bistro I go to quite often,' Theo was explaining. 'We go back a long way.'

'Oh, yes? How's that?' She wondered whether she might be able to sneak into the bathroom at the 'little French bistro' and do something with her hair, somehow glue it into submission.

'I helped him out a long time ago—financed him for the restaurant he wanted to open.'

'I knew you had a soft side!' Heather exclaimed impulsively, smiling at him.

Good Lord, Theo thought, the woman needed protecting from her own good nature!

'It was a sensible business arrangement,' Theo corrected, not much liking the image of him as having a *soft side*. If he had, he'd certainly never seen evidence of it, nor had any of those kings of finance who deferred to him the minute he opened his mouth. 'To dispel the myth, I made money out of the deal.'

'But I'm sure you would have invested in him even if you hadn't thought that you were going to. I guess that's what friendship's all about, isn't it?'

'I really have not given it much thought,' Theo said deflatingly. 'We are here.' He nodded as the car slowed down, and Heather glanced around to see that the little bistro was more of a chic restaurant—the sort of place that gathered trendy people who all sat around with glasses of white wine looking at everybody else.

She groaned aloud and shot him a frantic look.

'I can't go in there.'

'Why not?' Theo asked with a trace of irritation. He was beginning to wonder what demonic urge had impelled him into taking this dippy woman out. Yes, sure he was concerned by her ominous remarks about her future job—but, really, what business was it of his? Adults chose to do what they wanted to do with their lives. He decided right there and then that this would be his one truly good deed for the year.

'Look at me!' Heather squeaked, her face flushed with panic.

Theo looked. 'No one will pay you the slightest bit of attention.' That was the best he could do at consoling her without resort to outright lying.

'*Everyone* is going to look!' Heather contradicted in a high voice. 'I mean, just look at the people in there.' The wide goldfish-bowl-style restaurant offered an obliging view of a crowd of people smartly dressed and relaxing in an atmosphere of self-congratulation. They seemed to be making the statement that they were all beautiful, and thank goodness for that.

The car had now stopped and Theo's chauffeur had smoothly moved round to the passenger door, which he was opening for her.

Next to Theo, Heather felt even more of an embarrassment. She raised imploring eyes to him and he shook his head impatiently.

'You're too self-conscious about your appearance.'

'That's all right for *you* to say,' she informed him. 'You happen to be blessed with amazing good looks.'

'Do you always say what's on your mind?' Theo asked, a little taken aback by her blunt statement.

Heather ignored that. She was too busy hovering. He had to propel her through the door, and he might not notice a thing, but she certainly did. All those faces turned in their direction. The women sniggered, she was certain of it, before feasting their eyes on the man by her side.

The men shot her quick disparaging looks, and then they, too, looked at Theo, wondering whether they should recognise him. Heather felt worse than invisible. Indeed, invisible would have been a much more acceptable option. As it was, she stared down at the shiny wooden floor which made the most of highlighting her practical line in footwear.

'We're over there,' Theo murmured, bending down. 'Would you like me to lead you or are you prepared to look up and make your way to the table unaided?'

'Very funny,' Heather whispered back at him. 'Do you notice how everyone's staring at me, wondering what on earth I'm doing here?'

'No one's staring at you.'

'Well, they *were*,' Heather informed him,

reaching her chair with deep relief and sinking into it.

'Your mother has a lot to blame herself for in letting whatever complexes you have about your sister get out of hand.' He picked up the menu on the table but gave it only a scant perusal, obviously knowing in advance what he intended to order.

Heather leaned forward and looked at him earnestly. 'It wasn't Mum's fault that she happened to give birth to a swan and an ugly duckling.'

'Point proved. Is she aware that you constantly make comparisons between yourself and your sister?'

'Mum died seven years ago.' She waited for the meaningless expressions of regret but none were forthcoming. Instead, Theo held her gaze thoughtfully before giving her a quick nod. 'She was ill for about two years before she finally passed away. That's why I never finished my education. I needed to get working.'

'And what was your sister doing at the time?'

'Claire was in London, doing an acting course and some waitressing.'

'And you were left no assets that would have helped you with your own ambitions?' Against his will, he was curious about the dynamics of her family. Without looking away from her, he ordered a bottle of wine and the fish of the day, which she ordered as well.

Heather flushed. 'Claire needed what little there was far more than I did at the time. She promised that when she made it big she would pay me back—not that the money ever mattered. Mum was gone and I didn't really care about dividing what she'd left us, which wasn't very much anyway.'

'And has she made it big?' Theo asked casually, knowing what answer he would receive. Sure enough, it was no surprise to discover that dreams of stardom were languishing across the Atlantic. No surprise either to discover that the money had never managed to wing its way back to its original owner, who seemed stunningly content with the situation.

'So you are happy to compare yourself unfavourably to someone whose only claim to fame apparently lies in her looks?' Theo mused over a glass of wine.

'She also happens to be a very warm person,' Heather defended hotly. Mostly, she conceded to herself, when she was getting her own way. Her selfishness had always been a combination of infuriating and endearing. It had been hard to lose her temper with Claire, and the few times that she had she had met with a brick wall of plaintive incomprehension. 'Anyway, I don't *compare* myself to Claire. I just admire her looks. Don't you have brothers you sometimes compare yourself to?' It was such a ridiculous notion that she couldn't help but grin. 'No. I can't picture you comparing yourself unfavourably to anybody. You're way too self-confident for that. I guess you'd expect people to compare themselves to *you*.'

'No siblings,' Theo informed her flatly, his tone of voice warning her away from any further probing into his personal life, but Heather was gazing at him thoughtfully.

'That's very sad for you. I know that Claire doesn't live here, but it's just good knowing that she's with me in spirit, so to speak. What about your parents? Where do they live? Over here? They must be very proud of you, what with you being so successful in your job…'

Women didn't make a habit of probing into Theo's personal life. In fact, women knew when to back off without having to be told. Something in his expression had always been very good at warning them about the boundaries he laid down. He wined them and dined them and treated them with extravagant gestures that were wildly out of most people's orbit. In return he asked only for relationships without complications. His life was hectic enough without having to deal with demands from the opposite sex.

Heather didn't appear to have the correct instincts warning her to drop the subject. In fact, she was looking at him with the keen enthusiasm of a puppy dog waiting for a treat.

Just as well she was of no interest to him sexually. Theo was convinced that if you fed women with too much personal information, it engendered illusions of permanence. They thought that they had somehow crawled under your skin and were therefore in the right position to stage a complete takeover.

Since this woman was not in the category of a fisherman trawling a net in the hope of netting the fish, he didn't immediately succumb to the automatic instinct to shut down. Instead, he returned her gaze and shrugged.

'My father died when I was a boy and my

mother does not live over here. She lives in Greece.'

'Which, of course, is where you're from…'

Theo permitted himself a faint smile. 'Why *of course*…?'

'Oh, all those stereotypes of Greek men being tall, dark and handsome.' Heather grinned at the bemused expression on his face. She was just teasing, but she wondered how many times in his life he had ever been teased. 'Does your mother come and visit you often?'

'You ask a lot of questions.'

Their food arrived and was placed in front of them; their glasses were refilled with wine which Heather felt quite free to drink considering she was now out of a job.

'People have interesting stories. How else do you find out who they are if you don't ask questions?' Her appetite, which should have been sated after the sandwiches, stirred into life. Naturally she wasn't going to guzzle the lot, but it wasn't often that she found herself sitting in a restaurant of this calibre. Somehow it would have seemed rude to be dismissive of the food.

'So does she?' Heather persisted.

'What are you talking about?'

'Your mother. Does she come over and visit?'

Theo shook his head in pure exasperation. 'Occasionally,' he finally conceded. 'She visits my country house, and when she does I commute to London. She hates the city. In fact, she has never been here. There—satisfied?'

Heather nodded. *For the moment*, she wanted to say, before remembering that there would be no more moments, that in fact she was only here because he felt duty-bound to send her on her way with a bit more concern than he would probably otherwise have shown because he had effectively cost her her cleaning job. Which suddenly brought her back down to earth and the reality of losing an income, small though it was, which was necessary to her. She closed her knife and fork on the half-eaten plate of food and cupped her chin in one hand.

'You're finished?' Theo asked in amazement.

Heather felt a little jab of hurt coil deep inside her. Through the shield of her naturally sunny disposition she suddenly had a bleak vision of an alternative reality. The reality that was coldly pointing out that while she had nurtured pleasant fantasies about this tall, aggressively handsome man, while she had always made sure to clean his floor when she knew that he was going to be around, he had never once glanced in her direction—would not have recognised her if she had landed opposite him on a desert island. And while she luxuriated in the thrill of being in his company now, unexpected as it was, the thrill was not mutual. To him she was nothing but an overweight woman whose company he was probably itching to get away from.

'Did you think that I would carry on eating till I exploded?' Heather said, far more sharply than she had intended. She softened her uncharacteristically sarcastic reply with a rueful smile. 'Sorry, I was just thinking about what I shall do now that I no longer have a job to go to in the evenings.'

'I can't believe that you really have to hold down two jobs to survive. Surely you can cut back on one or two luxuries…make ends meet that way…?'

Heather laughed. Rich, warm laughter that had a few heads turning in her direction.

'You don't live in the real world, Mr Miquel…'

'Theo…'

'Well, you don't. I don't *have* any luxuries to cut

back on. Friends come over for meals and we watch television and maybe drink a couple of bottles of wine on a Saturday night, and in summer we go on picnics in the park. I don't do theatres or restaurants or even cinemas very often. Actually, I don't have an awful lot of free time anyway, which is probably a good thing when it comes to balancing my finances...' The look of horror on his face was growing by the second, but Heather was unfazed by that. Of course he wouldn't understand the world she lived in. Why should he? She probably only had a vague inkling of his. 'I prefer to save up for my course rather than blow money on clothes and entertainment.'

'And I thought being young was all about being reckless,' Theo drawled. With a spurt of surprise, he realised that he was having fun. Not quite the same fun that he normally had in the company of a woman, but he felt invigorated. Maybe his jaded palette needed novelty more often.

Heather lifted one shoulder dismissively. 'Maybe it is, if you can support a reckless lifestyle. Anyway, I'm not a reckless kind of person.'

'Then perhaps you should reconsider your job with this man...'

'Tom?' She looked at him in surprise. 'What's so reckless about working behind a bar a few nights every week? Just so long as I laugh a lot and chat to the punters, Tom will be more than happy with me.'

Theo looked down and did a rapid rethink on his original assumption, which seemed ridiculous now that he thought about it. 'Long hours?' was all he said, and she nodded.

'Very long and very tiring, which was why I turned down his offer all those months ago. But needs must. There aren't that many jobs a girl can do at night, and I can't fit anything else into my days.' She sighed. How helpful it would have been if Claire had been true to her word and sent back some of that money she had borrowed all that time ago. But it had been two months since she had spoken to her sister, and a lot longer since they had physically met up. It would be crazy when contact was so limited and precious, to start asking for her loan back.

'Anyway, no point moaning about all of that.' She smiled. 'The food was delicious. Thank you. I'm glad I came.'

'Even though you couldn't bear the thought of everyone staring at you?' He poured her another glass of wine, finishing the bottle, and wondered whether he should order another. If novelty had been what he was after, then he had certainly found it in this woman who was prepared to eat and drink without fear of the consequences. He also realised that it would be no hardship to prolong the evening a bit. After all, his current girlfriend was no longer around, and issues of work would wait until the morning, when he would return to his office to complete what he had started.

'More wine?' he asked, signalling to the waiter as he waited for her response.

Heather's face felt flushed. In fact, she felt quite warm, and would have removed her jumper but for the fact that the old tee shirt she was wearing underneath was even more of an eyesore than the thick grey sweater she had hurriedly stuck on when she had left the house earlier in the evening.

'Aren't I keeping you from something?' She looked at him earnestly.

'Like what?'

'Oh, I don't know. Don't you have somewhere to go? A date or something?'

'My date cancelled on me when I told her that I was running late.'

So that had been the urgent phone call which she had glimpsed out of the corner of her eye. Heather felt a rush of guilt and she reddened.

'That's awful!' She half stood up but he waved her back down, nodding at the waiter to pour the wine he had ordered. 'I can't be the cause of a row between you and your girlfriend. I'm sorry.'

'Sit back down,' Theo ordered, amused at her attack of conscience. 'You simply helped along the inevitable, if it's any consolation. Sit! People will stare. You don't want that, do you?'

Heather grudgingly took her seat, but her eyes were still anxiously focused on his face. 'What do you mean?' She gulped a mouthful of wine and then pushed the glass away from her.

'I mean—' he leant towards her '—I can see the group of people behind you, and they're just waiting to see if you're about to commit social suicide by causing a scene…'

'That's not what I meant!'

'I'm aware of that.'

'Oh!' She pushed some flyaway hair out of her face. 'Then what *did* you mean? About me helping along the inevitable? Were you going to dump her?'

'Sooner or later.' He sprawled back into his chair, folded his arms and stared at her transparently distraught face. Who would have imagined that the girl cleaning his office would have proved such a refreshing companion for the evening? He could hardly believe it himself.

'Oh.' Heather fell back on the single word. 'Why would she break up with you just because you were running late?' She frowned, puzzled. Yes, relationships could be transitory, but wasn't that taking it too far? She herself had only been in one long-standing relationship and even when they had both reached the point of recognising that things weren't going anywhere between them they had still taken many long evenings to finally cut the ties. 'And why would you have dumped her sooner or later? Weren't you serious about her?'

That, as far as Theo was concerned, was one question too far. He called for the bill and then leant forward, resting his elbows on the table.

'I think we've reached the point where you're asking about things that are none of your business.'

For a few charged moments Heather glimpsed the man everyone tiptoed around. The man with the steel hand in the velvet glove. She shrugged. 'Okay. I apologise. Sometimes I talk too much.'

'Sometimes you do,' Theo agreed unsmilingly. He settled the bill and, eager to return their last snatches of conversation to a less tense footing, Heather smiled brightly.

'I would offer to pay my way, but my finances…'

'Can barely run to a cinema show. I know.' He stood up and wondered again why such an ungainly girl would wear clothes that deliberately emphasised her girth.

Heather stood up quickly, too quickly, because suddenly the effects of having drunk too much of the very cold, very good white wine took their toll and she teetered slightly on her feet.

The ground had definitely felt more stable when she was sitting down.

And now she had to make her way across the even more crowded room.

'That's the problem with good wine,' Theo said lazily. 'Too easy to drink.' He moved over to where she was standing in panicked indecision and slipped his arm around her waist.

That contact seemed to electrify every inch of her body. She was aware of the heated racing of her pulses and a deep, steady throb that began somewhere in the pit of her stomach and flooded outwards, obliterating every ounce of common sense in its path.

A vague girlish crush…one night talking, the briefest of touches that meant absolutely zero to him…and she felt her head spinning like a woman in love.

She barely heard him talking to her as he ushered her through the room and out towards the exit, pausing *en route* to exchange a few pleasantries with Henri, who had materialised out of thin air and found time for banter even though he clearly had plenty of work to do.

Lord, but she wanted to curve her body into his! Had she ever felt this way with Johnny? She couldn't remember. She didn't think so.

As soon as they were outside he released her, and she took a couple of steps back, just to recover from that giddy sensation. The cold air was good. As was the safe, comforting bulk of her coat, which he had somehow managed to get her into.

His chauffeur was parked a few metres up, but

before he started walking her towards the car Heather looked at him and gave a watery smile.

'I'll be fine to make my way back from here,' she said, enunciating every word very carefully. She stuck her hands firmly into the deep pockets of her coat and clenched her fists.

'Don't be ridiculous. Where do you live?'

'Honestly. I'm fine. You've done too much already.' She was aware that there was just the smallest hint of her words being slurred. When he placed his hand on her elbow she knew that she would capitulate.

'You've gone very quiet...'

'I feel a bit wobbly...tired...' As soon as she was in the car she rested her head back and closed her eyes. She was dimly aware of giving Theo her address, and the next time she opened her eyes it was to find that they had arrived at the house which she shared with four other girls, all of whom were out. For the first time she realised that she must be the only person under the age of twenty-five, single and in London, who wasn't out doing something on a Friday night. Except she *had* done something!

He walked her to the door, took her bag from her

when she couldn't locate her keys and managed to find them. This after pulling out everything bar the kitchen sink from her voluminous sack. When he stepped inside the house Heather didn't protest. Yes, he had done his duty, and he was keen to be off, but, no, she didn't want him to leave. Not just yet. Not when she wouldn't be seeing him again.

'Would you like some coffee?' Heather asked awkwardly.

'How many of you share this place?'

'Four.' She hiccupped, and covered her mouth with her hand.

'I think you probably need the coffee more than I do. Go and sit down and I'll make you some.'

Well, Theo reasoned, his evening had gone wildly wrong starting from the moment he'd heard that crash outside his office, so why not wrap it up doing something he rarely did? Waiting on a woman who was the worse for wear and had probably collapsed into a snoring heap on her sofa?

Theo wasn't a brutish male chauvinist. However, he had been spoilt by the attention lavished on him by members of the opposite sex. His looks, his charisma and his vast wealth had always been a powerful magnetic pull for women who heeded his slightest whim. He had never particularly had to put himself out. In fact, he couldn't recall the last time he had taken care of a woman in the manner in which he was now taking care of the one who had fallen asleep beside him in the car when he had been in the middle of a sentence.

He made his way to the back of the house, observing the chaos in which four people apparently lived with no pressing desire to tidy up behind themselves. The kitchen sported the detritus of breakfast eaten on the run and not cleared away. Jumpers were slung in odd places and shoes were randomly scattered. On the window ledge a row of cards suggested a birthday had come and gone.

Coffee made, he reached the sitting room to find that Heather had fallen asleep. She had stripped off her jumper and was sprawled on the sofa with one arm raised, half covering her face and dipping over the arm of the chair.

She had kicked off her shoes, revealing thick grey socks.

Theo stood for a few seconds, drawing in a sharp breath, because the shapeless figure wasn't quite as shapeless as he had imagined. Her breasts

were big, succulently generous, but there was proportion to her body and the sliver of skin he
glimpsed where the tee shirt rose up was surprisingly firm.

He rubbed his eyes to dispel the uneasy sensation of staring at her, and the even more uneasy
suspicion that he would have liked to move closer
so that he could appreciate those curves a bit more.

Without waking her up, he deposited the coffee
on the table by the sofa and, after a few seconds'
hesitation, pulled out his pen and hunted around
for some paper. He wasn't going to wake her, but
walking away without saying goodbye somehow
felt wrong. So he jotted down a couple of lines,
wishing her luck in getting a new job, then he
left, resisting the terrible urge to look back over
his shoulder at her softly breathing body.

Once outside, he laughed at the insanity that had
possessed him for a few fleeting seconds. He had
looked at her and *had been turned on*! He almost
called Claudia, knowing that some sweet talk
would have her running back into his arms, but
instead he switched off his mobile phone and forced
his highly disciplined brain to concentrate on the
work he had had to defer to the following morning.

Heather, surfacing the next day to the sounds of one of her room-mates clattering about in the kitchen, had a few seconds of blissful oblivion during which she imagined the sounds to be Theo, making her that cup of coffee.

The cup of coffee lying cold on the table by her. Next to a note which she now read. It said nothing at all. A few polite words scribbled down before he left the house, doubtless relieved that there was no need for him to continue the charade of entertaining her.

Heather sat up and buried her head in her hands. He hadn't woken her up! She had fallen asleep and lost her opportunity to spend a few more minutes in his company.

The sun seemed to have gone out of her life. It was only when, after a week, one of her friends in the house mentioned it that Heather gave herself a stiff lecture. Moping around over a man she had known for roughly three hours was insane.

'Am I insane?' she asked her reflection. 'No. Because you know,' she added, wagging her finger censoriously at herself, 'only a complete loony would lose sleep over a man like Theo!'

She pulled herself together and accepted the job at Tom's pub. It was, as she had predicted, hard work but sociable, and was suited to her temperament. The hours might have been longer, and her exhaustion levels might have been higher, but she was at least eating regularly, and she took Fridays off. Theo's remark about being young and enjoying life had stuck in her head.

Not, even after six weeks, that any of those fun-packed Friday evenings with her friends could compare to that one night that had sprung from nothing and disappeared before she could hold onto it.

And his image kept slipping into her head. She couldn't seem to help it. One minute she would be laughing at something and the next minute there he was, released from the restraints she kept trying to put on him. She went to bed with him at night and woke up to him the following morning, and she just couldn't help it. It was involuntary. The man haunted her.

Of course it would end. Time had a wonderful way of healing, and she cheerfully resigned herself to due process. She was so resigned, in fact, that when, two months after she had last laid eyes on him, she picked up her telephone to hear his voice on the other end, she almost didn't recognise it.

Then she sat down, flapping her arm madly so that Beth would turn the television down, which she did, making sure she remained where she was to overhear the conversation. Heather could feel her heart start racing. He had managed to get her name from the firm of cleaners she had worked for, apparently. Heather assumed his influence must have unlocked her personnel file, since its contents were confidential. Not that she cared. She just wanted him to tell her why he had called.

'I have a proposition to put to you,' he finally said, when pleasantries had been exhausted.

'Really?' She tried to keep the stomach-turning curiosity out of her voice.

'My housekeeper has gone. Her sister in Scotland has fallen ill and needs looking after. The job has become vacant and I thought of you.' He briefly explained what it entailed. It could even, he informed her, be a live-in post. His apartment had a separate wing and he was rarely there anyway. He preferred to spend as many of his free weekends as he could in the country. He told her how much she would be earning and the figure made her gasp. It was far and away more than she was currently earning with both her jobs combined. She would be able to save and, if she decided to live in, would be able to afford her course within months, instead of the tortuous years she had anticipated.

Not that financial considerations played much of a part in her decision.

'I accept,' she told him promptly, making him smile at the other end of the line. 'Just tell me when you want me to start...'

CHAPTER THREE

'So,' BETH said sternly, 'what happens next?'

Eighteen months on and they were sitting in the usual place they met, an all-day French wine bar and restaurant which never seemed particularly bothered about serving cappuccinos to people who had zero intention of eating but would still manage to occupy valuable seats for hours at a stretch.

Heather bit her lower lip nervously, because she knew exactly what was coming. She managed to buy herself a few seconds of thinking time by taking a sip of her coffee, but the question was still there when she met her friend's concerned, probing brown eyes.

'What do you mean?' she dodged unsuccessfully.

To start with Beth had been overjoyed at her friend's sudden run of good luck. To be asked to do something as undemanding as looking after a house that would be very clean most of the time anyway, considering its owner wasn't often there, at a salary that was way over the going rate, sure beat the hell out of working in Tom's rowdy pub till all hours of the morning. Giving up the assistant teaching job would be a wrench, but, heck, she would be able to complete her course and then get started on the career ladder.

As far as Beth was concerned, a woman was defined by her career. She herself had wanted to be a lawyer from the age of five, if she was to be believed, and had got on with turning her dream into reality without ever deviating from her route.

Heather deeply admired her friend's ambitious streak. So much so that she had tried very hard in the beginning not to let on that her real reason for accepting Theo's generous offer was her own inarticulated need to be near him. But, not being secretive by nature, she had soon lapsed into easy confidences, and ever since had had to endure her friend's occasionally withering remarks about being used.

'I *mean*,' Beth said, leaning forward with the concerned frown of one friend trying to impart to another friend what should have been self-evident, 'now that your course has finished, are you going to move out and get a job with that publishing company? The one you sent your application off to? You *did* send that application off, didn't you?'

Heather wilted in the face of this direct line of questioning and mumbled something about needing to add a few finishing touches to it. In truth, the envelope had been lying in her bag for a fortnight while she fought off the sickening prospect of leaving behind a situation that was going nowhere but happened to be working very nicely for her.

While she continued to fan the flames of her infatuation, Theo was as far removed from being interested in her sexually as he ever had been. Theirs was an evolving situation. She had evolved into emotional dependency and he had evolved into having the perfect housekeeper. Indeed, her housekeeping duties were now virtually non-existent. She did some light cleaning, mostly in her own wing, some even lighter cooking to accommodate him when he happened to be in for supper, but mostly she had become a curious mixture of out-of-hours secretary and general do-it-all.

He talked to her about work issues, no longer reminding her that everything he told her was always in the strictest confidence. She'd used to laugh at his frowning secrecy, gently informing him that she personally didn't know a single person who would have been remotely interested in offshore deals involving companies they had never heard of. He would watch her as she pottered around his kitchen, chatting about her friends and what they got up to.

He found her relaxing and amusing and, more importantly, undemanding. Unlike the women he continued to wine and dine, she showed none of the clinginess that some of them displayed, and she had never nurtured ambitions beyond her reach. In his eyes, they had the perfect relationship. He paid her handsomely, and had increased her already generous salary every three months in direct proportion to the level of duties she took on. In return she helped him in ways far beyond what he would have expected his own secretary at work to do.

She never minded running through e-mails with him, or typing up letters that had to be done late at night after he had left the office. Nor did she balk at buying expensive jewellery for girlfriends, or even ordering the customary bunch of red roses he would have delivered when a relationship was nearing the end of its natural life span.

On a couple of occasions, when he had been out of the country and way too busy to shop, she had even purchased gifts for his mother, which she'd had couriered over to Greece. She could be relied upon to choose just the right thing. He should know. He had seen the reactions of the recipients.

There was nothing Beth could tell her that Heather didn't already know. This time, though, it was different. She had finished her illustration course and had come top of her class. She no longer needed to save madly. In fact Theo's generous salary, and the fact that she paid no rent—at his insistence—meant that she had managed to foot the bill for the course, buy all her coursework material, even take herself off on various excursions to exhibitions of interest, and still have money in the bank. Not enough to put down for buying her own place, but more than enough to rent somewhere on her own.

Every word Beth was telling her now made sense. Confronted by too much of the truth to be palatable, Heather took refuge in vague answers.

'I actually know of an apartment...' Beth casually announced, glancing at her watch because her lunch hour had extended well beyond its time limit. 'It's in my block. It's not as big as mine, just the one bedroom, but you'll love it, and you wouldn't have someone knocking on your door in the late hours of the night, expecting you to fling on a dressing gown and follow him so that you can transcribe some letter that he could easily get his secretary to do the next day...'

But I never mind doing that, Heather wanted to say. She knew better, though. So she nodded distantly and tried to look enthusiastic. 'I could have a look...' she compromised.

Beth took that for a definite *yes* and stood up and reached for her briefcase. 'Good. Let me know when you're free and I'll sort out an appointment for you. But I'm telling you now that you won't be able to sit around and think about things, because it'll be snapped up in no time at all.' As if aware of the preaching tone of her voice, she grinned sheepishly and gave Heather a friendly hug. 'I care about you,' she said.

'I know.'

'And I hate to think of you languishing in that

man's house, desperately waiting for him to notice you while you busy yourself doing his dirty errands.'

'I don't—'

'Of course you do!' Beth cut short the protest briskly. Heather, she had decided long ago, had an amazing knack for justifying Theo's bad behaviour and her responses to it. She had met him a few times in the past and knew, realistically, that hell would freeze over before he looked at Heather in any way aside from that of one lucky employer who had a doting employee at his beck and call. He liked his women tall, thin and vacant. Heather resoundingly didn't fit into any of those categories, and as far as Beth was concerned she let herself down by feeding the illusion that one day he might see her with different eyes.

'I'm off now, darling. You take care—and *phone me*. Okay?'

'Okay,' Heather agreed readily, not quite dismissing the option of moving out, but not giving it much importance either.

Fate had brought her together with Theo, in a manner of speaking, and fate wasn't quite ready to take her away.

But the application in her handbag, the possibility of a flat and Beth's stern little talk did have her thinking as she made her way back to Theo's place.

On the way back she stopped off and bought a few things from the delicatessen at the corner— things she knew he would like. He would be away for the weekend, but tonight he would be in. She would make him some spaghetti Bolognese, to which he was very partial.

As she approached the apartment block she tried not to think of his weekend activities. He was seeing yet another of his impossibly beautiful brunettes. This one was called Venetia, and she suited the name. She was almost as tall as he was in heels, only wore designer clothes, and on the one occasion she had met Heather had treated her with the slightly disdainful superiority of someone very beautiful in the presence of a troll.

That Heather was jealous was something she would never have revealed to Theo.

But, on top of everything else, it filtered into her system now like poison.

It was no longer enough to content herself with the silly delusion that enjoying him was enough. Yes, she found him endlessly fascinating, with his endearing arrogance, his sharp wit and his moments of real thoughtfulness. But was it really enough?

She had completed her course two weeks ago, and in its wake the grinding clang of time was left marching on, reminding her, in the sudden void, that she had a life to be getting on with—and not a life that revolved around one man who really didn't pay her a scrap of attention even though she knew, in some inexplicable way, that she was virtually indispensable to him.

Or are you? a nasty little voice in her head said, making her pause in her tracks. *You'd like to think you are, but don't we all believe the things we want to believe and discard the rest?*

It was with a heavy heart that Heather walked up to his apartment. She had started that as a form of exercise over the past few weeks—as a way of counteracting her love of chocolate and all things sweet and therefore calorie laden.

Theo lived on the top floor of a high-specification block of penthouse apartments in the very heart of Knightsbridge. Typically, his was by far the largest, encompassing the entire upper floor of the building. It was as big as any conventional house, although laid out in a contem-

porary fashion, and he had not stinted in its dec-
oration. In fact, he had told her, as she'd traipsed
her way through in awestruck silence on her very
first day, he had simply employed the top designer
in London to come in and have his way with it.
His only constraints had involved colour—as little
of it as possible—and no plants which would
require looking after.

Over the months Heather had done nothing
about the colour, but she *had* brought in plants,
which she religiously tended.

She had also brightened up the walls with some
of her illustrations, unruffled by Theo's initial
grunting response and then gratified by his occasional appreciative remarks.

Her interest in hanging a few more, which she
had been looking forward to choosing from her
portfolio, had been squashed under her uncustomary downward spiral of thoughts.

She let herself into the apartment, dumped the
food in the fridge and, still reeling from the depress-
ing effect of Beth's opinions, headed for the shower.

It was wonderfully refreshing. Although
summer was on its last legs, and had been a particularly uneventful one even by English stan-

dards, it had been a muggy day and she had built up a healthy sweat trekking up the flights of stairs with a fairly heavy carrier bag.

The sound of the doorbell being rung insistently only just managed to penetrate the sound of the shower and the clamour of her thoughts.

Of course it wouldn't be Theo. Theo never, but never, got back before seven in the evening. He also possessed his own key, which he would never be scatty enough to misplace. But even so...who else could it be? The porter on the ground floor would never allow any salesperson to go up the elevator. It would have been more than his life was worth. Very rich people hugged their privacy and would have been horrified at the thought that any old person could come knocking on their door demanding their attention. In fact, sightings of neighbours were few and far between. Heather was convinced that the super-rich possessed some kind of special radar that warned them when to venture out of their apartments and when not to.

She felt her heartbeat quicken at the thought that she might open the door to see Theo standing there.

It wasn't Theo. And it wasn't a salesperson, unlikely as that option had been. It was a short, dark-haired woman in her sixties, with a face that should have been fierce but just looked exhausted.

Heather didn't know who was more surprised to see whom. They broke the silence at the same time, one speaking voluble Greek, the other stuttering out a bewildered request for some identity. Eventually, they both fell silent once more, until Heather said, her natural friendliness kicking in, 'I'm sorry, but would you mind telling me who you are? It's just that...well...not many people are allowed up unless they're expected...' She smiled to offset any offence that might have been taken. Not having had time to change into anything else, she clutched the cord of her bathrobe tightly around her and was self-consciously aware of bright black eyes appraising her.

'Who are *you*?' The woman peered around Heather. 'Where is my son? Is my son here? The man at the desk said that there would be someone to open up for me. I thought he was talking about Theo. Where is he? Who are you?'

Heather gaped. Theo had mentioned his mother now and again—the mother for whom he had the deepest respect and admiration, the mother who never ventured to London because the crowds confused her.

'Please—come in, Mrs Miquel.' A shy smile. 'I'm so glad to meet you. I'm Heather...'

'Heather? Heather who? Theo never mentioned a Heather to me, but then my son never talks about his girlfriends. I was beginning to think he had none! Or maybe too many...eh?' She bustled into the apartment and immediately headed for the sofa, where she sat down with a sigh of relief. 'Come over here, child. Let me see you.'

'Oh, but you've got the wrong—'

'Shh!' Theo's mother placed one finger commandingly over her lips. 'Humour an old woman who has been praying so long for her son to find a nice girl to settle down with. And this could not have come at a better time for me, my child. Yes. You look plump and well fed.'

'I'm on a diet...' Heather mumbled, aghast at the other woman's misconceptions and determined to set things straight. 'Well, soon will be...cabbages...soup... I'll shed pounds... But, you know, I think... Well...I'm sorry to disappoint you...but...'

'Disappointed? Of course I am not disappointed, my child...!' The old face suddenly lit up with a smile and Heather helplessly smiled back. 'Theo likes to think that I am old-fashioned…maybe that is why he did not tell me about you…he thought that I would disapprove of you two living together…'

'No, Mrs Miquel…' Heather urgently positioned herself on the sofa, acutely conscious that her state of dress was doing nothing to further the truth. 'I mean, we *are* living together…*technically*…'

'And, while I am an old woman, I am not that old that I do not realise how times have changed. In my day—well…we did things differently. But that is not to say that I do not understand how young people do things…' She unexpectedly reached out to cup the side of Heather's face with her hand. 'I am just happy that my beloved Theo has found someone, and I can tell you are a kind person. It is in your eyes.'

Heather wondered how kindness could be so easily confused with panic.

'And you must not call me Mrs Miquel, my child. My name is Litsa.'

'Theo didn't say anything about you coming over…'

'I had hoped to…' Her face fell into anxious

lines of worry. 'It is best if I explain to him in person... Now, I am tired...perhaps you could call Theo...explain that I am here...?'

'Of course!' Since Litsa's eyelids were fluttering shut, and her strength was clearly sapped, Heather didn't feel it appropriate to embark on a lengthy explanation of how it was that she came to be occupying Theo's flat, currently dressed in a bathrobe, and what her real role was. She decided that it was perhaps best to leave that little nugget of disillusionment to Theo.

In the meantime she would escort Litsa to one of the spare rooms, make sure that she was settled into bed, and bring her something to eat—although, after that first outburst of curiosity, she now seemed to have wilted.

Thankfully, the sprawling apartment had several spare bedrooms, two with *en suite* bathrooms, and Heather showed her to one of these. How she had managed to accomplish a trip to London was a mystery, because she suddenly seemed very fragile, like a piece of china that could be easily broken. She was asleep before Heather had finished removing her jacket and shoes. Making as little noise as possible, she closed the curtains and tucked her underneath the covers.

However, she felt sure that anyone who wasn't stone deaf would have heard her heart beating like a steam engine.

Her fingers were trembling as she dialled Theo's mobile phone. He answered immediately, his tone of voice implying that she had interrupted him in the middle of something important. She took a deep breath and spoke quickly, just in case he decided to hang up on her without giving her the benefit of the doubt. When it came to matters of work Theo did not possess a sense of humour. Heather had worked sufficiently with him to have spotted the change that came over him the minute he lost himself in anything to do with his job.

'What are you talking about?' he snapped. 'I can't understand a word you're saying.'

'I'm saying that *your mother is here*, Theo.'

'Hold on.' There was a few seconds of silence, then he was back on the line. 'Now speak.'

Heather knew that her words were leaping over each other. Several times he had to ask her to slow down. No, she didn't know *why* Litsa had shown up…but she was asleep now and *he had to drop whatever he was doing and come back to the apartment immediately.*

There was nothing Theo hated more than any distraction from work, and right now he was in the middle of a high-level conference, but for the first time he felt something more powerful than the magnetic pull of his work. He felt fear. It fizzed in his blood like acid as he hurtled out of his office, urgently calling his chauffeur to have his car ready and waiting outside.

Typically for Heather, who had never learned the art of economising with her speech, she had babbled on in a confused manner about needing to set his mother straight about something or other, but he had barely heard. His brain had already leapt to possibilities that did not bear thinking about.

His mother *never* came to London, never mind without any prior warning. To have travelled over without first informing him was unthinkable.

Indeed, Theo could think of no reason why his mother should not have warned him of her arrival. He briefly wondered whether she *had*, whether he had misfiled the information somewhere in his head, but he immediately discounted that. He forgot nothing—and certainly nothing as important as his mother coming to England.

The car had not quite stopped before he was opening the passenger door and heading towards the apartment block.

He burst through the door of his apartment to find Heather anxiously waiting for him, dressed in her usual garb of leggings and a baggy tee shirt with broad stripes.

'She's sound asleep,' Heather said, leaping to her feet and catching him by the arm before he could storm into the bedroom to ask questions.

His eyes looked wild and she relaxed her hold into something more reassuring. 'Let me make you some coffee. We need to talk.'

For a few seconds she thought he was going to shrug her hand off and head for the bedroom, but instead he ran his fingers through his hair and nodded.

He watched as she meticulously made some coffee. Along with all the other amazing and under-used high-tech gadgets in his kitchen was a cappuccino maker which he had never learnt to use. Heather, ditzy as she was, had sussed it out in no time, and now she handed him a cup of frothy coffee and sat opposite him at the chrome and glass kitchen table.

'Is there a problem?' Theo demanded. 'My mother never makes unannounced visits to this country so I am assuming that there is. What exactly did she say?'

'You mean did she tell me why she had come over?'

'That's right. Did she?'

Heather shook her head slowly and tried to figure out how to break it to him that his mother had rushed into some pretty horrendous misconceptions. She had tried on the telephone but her words had come out all jumbled, and anyway he hadn't been listening. Even from the other end of the line she had managed to glean that much.

'Theo. Is she all right? I mean, physically? She looked a little…frail…'

Theo's eyes darkened and he leant towards her. 'Explain.'

'She just seemed delicate…'

'And you would have been able to see that all in the space of what…half an hour? Because you're not actually doing an art course at all? Because you're actually studying to become a doctor?' He gave a bark of laughter under which Heather could pick up the strains of fear and her eyes widened sympathetically.

Theo stood up abruptly and pushed his chair back, then he leaned both hands on the table and shot her a hard, cold look. 'And spare me the compassion. I'm not in the mood for it.'

'Okay.' She felt the sting of tears at the back of her eyes and bit her lip.

Theo looked at her downbent head and knew that he had been unnecessarily cruel, but the apology he felt obliged to offer refused to come to his lips. Did she have any idea how her passing glib remark had consolidated all the nebulous fears that had been swimming about in his head? He banged his fist on the table and Heather jumped.

'I'm sorry,' she whispered.

'Sorry about what?' Theo snarled back. 'About offering your opinion when it hasn't been asked for?'

'Sorry that you're scared.' She met his eyes bravely and was relieved when he at least deigned to sit back down. She had never seen him scared before, had never seen him even close to it. If he wanted to take it out on her, then so be it. Wasn't that what love was all about? And didn't she love him?

However, she instinctively knew that dwelling on it wasn't a good idea, so she gave him a watery smile and sighed.

'There's something else,' she volunteered tentatively. 'I did try explaining to you on the phone, but I'm not sure you understood what I was trying to say. You know how sometimes I say stuff and it doesn't come out the way I mean…'

In the face of this prosaic understatement Theo felt some of the tension drain away from him and he smiled grudgingly. 'I've noticed.'

'Well…when your mother rang the doorbell I was in the shower…'

Theo frowned and tried to make sense of this random statement. He couldn't, so he waited patiently for her to continue. Given sufficient time, Heather's ramblings usually led to a fairly coherent place.

'I know you're probably thinking that it was a pretty odd time to have a shower, in the middle of the afternoon, but I'd decided to climb the stairs with some shopping… Anyway… Yes, I was in the shower and I went to answer the door in my bathrobe…'

'Do you plan on getting to the point any time this year?'

'Forget about the bathrobe…it doesn't matter. The *point* is…and I know you're going to be angry at this but it *wasn't my fault*…your mother wasn't expecting to see me.'

'Why didn't she ask Hal to let her up if she wasn't expecting to find anyone in the apartment?'

'Because Hal told her that someone would be here…she just expected that someone to be *you*…'

'At four-thirty in the afternoon?'

Heather ignored this rhetorical question and fixed him with a pleading stare which immediately sent alarm bells clanging in his head.

'I'm afraid she got the wrong impression…'

'Got the wrong impression? What impression did she get?'

'That I was…somehow involved with you…'

'You *are* involved with me. You're my house-keeper, amongst other things.'

'Not that kind of involved, Theo. Involved,

involved. On a romantic level involved. As in your girlfriend.'

Theo's reaction was unexpected. He burst out laughing.

'I know it's incredible,' Heather said tightly. 'I know I'm not the sort of woman you would glance at twice…'

Theo stopped laughing and looked at her narrowly, faintly uneasy about her tone of voice, but she had already progressed to the main body of the story and he was now getting the picture loud and clear.

He had kept his mother in the dark about his frequent liaisons—half to protect her, half to spare himself the inevitable disappointment he knew he would read on her face—and now she had walked in on a woman in a bathrobe, sharing his apartment, and had jumped to all the wrong conclusions.

'But you told her the truth, didn't you?' he interrupted.

'I couldn't.'

'You couldn't? Run that by me, Heather. My mother starts telling you how pleased she is that her son has finally found himself a good woman and you *don't find it possible to point her in the right direction?*' He was beginning to wonder how a day at the office could end up going so monstrously wrong.

'She didn't let me get a word in edgeways, Theo, and then she just sort of…lost all her steam—as though energy had been drained out of her—and I just didn't have the heart to shake her and tell her that she'd made a mistake…'

'Well, I'll sort that out.' He took a sip of his coffee and regarded Heather over the rim of his cup. Heather? Girlfriend? Ridiculous notion. His eyes drifted over her face, with its finely defined features and expressive eyes, then downwards to the striped tee shirt that did absolutely nothing for her and seemed to belong to a range of clothing specifically chosen for that purpose.

Yes, sure, she might have a personality—quite a bit of a personality, as he had discovered over time—but personality wasn't high on Theo's list of desirable qualities in a woman.

'Shouldn't be a problem,' he continued.

'You mean because no one in their right mind would ever think that I might be attractive?' Heather heard the words come out of her with a start of surprise, and she carried on quickly, not giving him time to latch onto their significance. 'Perhaps you ought to go and check on her…she seems to have been asleep for a while…'

'Where did *that* come from?' Theo asked with a frown. Heather might not be a candidate for a modelling contract, but then again he had never once seen her succumb to any real insecurities about her appearance. She joked about her figure now and again, and always seemed to be on some diet or another, but that was as far as it went. 'Has some man insulted you?' He felt a flare of sudden overpowering rage.

'Don't be silly, Theo. I'm just…in a weird mood. Must be your mother showing up…'

Which brought him back to what his mother was doing here, and he nodded and stood up. 'I'm going to go and check on her.'

'Don't wake her up if she's still asleep,' Heather urged. 'She looked as though she needed the rest. Perhaps she came over here to relax.' That made no sense at all, but she couldn't bear to see the sudden lines of strain etched on his darkly handsome features. It was funny how successfully he had always managed to promote his own invincibility. To see him vulnerable hurt her in ways she couldn't define. Nor could she express how she felt, because he would have rejected her sympathy as fiercely as if she had offered him a cup of arsenic.

'You don't have to patronise me,' Theo said dryly, but at least, Heather thought, he wasn't angry, and she smiled.

'I do if it stops you worrying so much.'

'Why?'

'Because…' She felt *terra firma* begin to shift worryingly under her feet. 'Because I would do it for anyone.' Which was a version of the truth at any rate. 'I can't bear to see anyone hurting.'

'A good Samaritan?' Theo said, still looking at her intently. 'Well, now I'm going to see my mother, and I shall end up being the bad Samaritan when I inform her that her notions about us are a load of rubbish.' He laughed and shook his head, as if still incredulous that such an error of judgement might have been made in the first place.

It left Heather thinking how important it was now to leave. She couldn't blame Theo for the fact that he found any idea of them being connected romantically a complete joke. The joke, she miserably pondered, was on her. She had harboured a ridiculous unfounded infatuation with him virtually from the very first moment she had clapped eyes on him, sitting behind his desk, brow furrowed in concentration, barely aware of her existence as she cleaned around him. And that had eventually led her here, to his apartment, entrenched in feelings that would never be reciprocated. Beth had been right all along. She needed to control her life and set it in the direction she wanted to take—instead of passively allowing her emotions to dictate to her.

It all made perfect sense to her in the forty-five minutes she spent in the kitchen, waiting for Theo to emerge and wondering whether it was appropriate for her to wait at all.

When he eventually did come out, she knew from his expression that the news wasn't going to be good.

'I need something stronger than coffee,' was the first thing he said as he sat at the kitchen table and wearily pressed his thumbs on his eyes. 'And I suggest,' he added, 'that you have something as well.'

Occasionally Heather had wine with Theo when

she happened to have cooked for him, but actually she was on an alcohol-free diet, guaranteed to shed several pounds in combination with rigorous exercise—which she planned on getting down to very soon. The look on his face put paid to that. She poured them both a glass and sat down facing him.

'She did not want to worry me,' Theo said at last. 'The chest pains began a while ago, but she put it down to old age, wear and tear. Eventually, she made an appointment with her doctor, who referred her to his colleague in London, a specialist in heart surgery.'

Heather gasped. 'And you had no idea…?'

'If I had, do you think that I would have allowed her to carry that burden on her own?' Theo snapped irritably. She had tapped into his own dark guilt—guilt that he had been so wrapped up in his own fast-moving life that he barely surfaced to see what was going on around him. 'She took the private jet over to London, visited with the doctor, who did a few tests, and she was then told that flying back to Greece was not a realistic option. Which was when she decided to come here, to my flat. Which was when she met you…'

CHAPTER FOUR

HEATHER waited for an improvement on this flatly spoken statement, which had carried just a hint of accusation with it. None was forthcoming.

'Look,' she said, drawing in a deep breath, 'I've been thinking…and…' The prospect of saying goodbye loomed ahead of her like a yawning Black Hole, but she ducked down and ploughed on. 'And now your mother's here…and, well… *especially as she seemed to get the wrong impression of me*…it wouldn't be appropriate…for me to stay on here…' She could feel her cheeks reddening under his silent watchful gaze, and the wrenching in her gut as she absorbed the enormity of what she was doing. Not that it wasn't the *right* thing to do—because it absolutely was!

'I've finished my course now, and it's time I moved on…with a proper job. Not that it hasn't been great being here... Well, Beth has a flat in mind for me, actually...it's in the same block as hers. Just small, of course, because I won't be able to afford that much to start with...' As usual she could hear herself turning one small statement of fact into several bewildering thousands, and she forced herself to shut up and smile.

Theo shrugged. 'It is naturally up to you if you feel inclined to move out...'

Heather fought the undermining temptation to retract her rash statement and buy herself just a little more time, just a few more months. 'I think it's for the best,' she mumbled.

'So might it be. Just not yet.'

For a few wild seconds her heart leapt as she translated those three words into what she wanted to hear. *Need, love, want!* Then reality sank its teeth into her and she looked at him, bemused.

'Permit me to clarify,' he said, finishing his wine and helping himself to another glass. 'As I said, my mother has a heart problem. She's explained it to me as best as she can and it would appear that it is not life threatening. Of course I will talk to her consultant in depth about that.' He frowned, and Heather could read his thoughts as if they were written on his forehead in large neon lettering. She felt sorry for the consultant. 'But, at any rate, it is imperative that she is spared any stress.'

'Naturally,' Heather nodded, relieved. Things might have been a lot worse.

'Which brings me to you,' Theo said smoothly. He sat back and tapped the table with one thoughtful forefinger. 'My mother, as you pointed out, is under the illusion that we are involved with one another, that I have finally found the woman I want to settle down with. In her head, you are living in my apartment, and therefore we are conducting a serious relationship…'

'You mean *you haven't told her the truth*?'

'It was impossible,' Theo informed her flatly, and Heather gaped at him in consternation. 'She's in a very fragile state of health at the moment. If I tell her the truth, then there is no telling how it might affect her current situation.'

'But you have to!' Heather cried.

'Not necessarily.'

'Not necessarily? I plan on *moving out*, Theo! Don't you think she might suspect that something's not quite right when your so-called serious relationship rents a flat on the other side of town?

Anyway,' she continued, 'it wouldn't be right to deceive an old woman…'

'It wouldn't be right to burden her with stress she cannot handle…'

'How can you assume that your mother wouldn't be able to handle the truth, Theo?' She leaned forward, so that her hands were lying flat on the table between them. 'You're not thinking straight.'

'I know I'm not,' Theo said simply. 'But I'm afraid to take the chance.'

As easily as that he managed to slice through all her protests and appeal to her on the most basic of levels, and although there was absolute sincerity in his eyes, she wouldn't have been surprised if he had deliberately used the ploy because he knew her well enough to realise that her emotions were her downfall. This was a girl who sobbed during the sad bits in films, who would give her last coins to a busker on the underground and who continued to have faith in a sister who had taken her money and headed for the hills.

Theo watched the sudden indecision in her eyes and breathed an inward sigh of relief.

'It won't be for long,' he promised. 'A couple of

weeks—no more. Just until she's strong enough to travel back to Greece…'

'And you'll break it to her then…?'

'I'll break to her gently, over time. Put it this way, your role will soon be over. After that you can get your proper job and find your proper flat and start your proper life.' He didn't know why the thought of that made him ever so slightly angry, but it did. Since he didn't care to analyse the emotion, he let it go. There were far more pressing things to think about.

How easy it was for him to say that, Heather thought sadly. She could easily be replaced. There weren't many who would bite a hand willing to part with generous sums of money for very easy work.

She thought of the times when she had foolishly bought presents for his girlfriends, while the pain of being the helpful employee in the background had twisted inside her like a knife. Well, if she had thought that fate hadn't quite finished with her, how right she had been!

'I think I'll go to my room now,' Heather said, standing up. 'I'll come out a bit later, if your mother wakes up, but I'm not very hungry.'

'Another one of your crazy diets?' Theo asked, and she replied with a smile that was neither friendly nor hostile. She felt as though the stuffing had been knocked out of her. But before she could leave the room he was talking again, telling her as if it was the most normal thing in the world that his mother expected them to be sharing a bedroom.

Heather spun round and looked at him, aghast. '*Share a room*?' she squeaked, walking towards him. '*With you*?'

'It's a very big bedroom,' Theo said placatingly. 'With a sofa.'

'Out of the question!'

'Why?' He raised his eyebrows in what was the first indication of amusement since he had walked into the flat a couple of hours previously. 'What do you think I'm going to do?'

'I don't think *anything*!'

'Then why the sudden outburst?' he asked curiously. 'Unless you think I might be tempted to touch…?' A sudden image of her flashed through his head, a picture of her lying on the sofa many months ago, after he had delivered her back to the house she had been sharing at the time…lying with her hand flung back and her breasts, full and heavy, gently rising and falling as she breathed.

'It just doesn't seem right,' Heather muttered, blushing furiously. She could tell that he was laughing at her and was bitterly hurt and angry.

Theo's voice was more brusque than he intended. 'I know it's not ideal, but it won't be for long. Now, you'll have to clear your belongings into my bedroom—or at least some of them. Enough to…'

'Perpetuate the charade?' Heather heard herself say tightly. She couldn't remember ever speaking to him like that, with real anger in her voice, not even when she had been feeling angry inside. It was as though she was looking at herself for the first time and watching someone else—someone who had been prepared to do as he asked, like a puppy following its master, because the pure pleasure of being around him now and again had outweighed everything else. Every last ounce of common sense.

Now fate had played one last trick on her, and she was being punished in the most cruel way possible.

'Why can't you get Venetia to come and stay with you?' Heather asked in a more normal voice.

'That way, at least you won't be lying.' And that, more than anything else, would force her to make a decision and move out, because knowing that he was in his room with his current girlfriend would have taken the knife-twisting a step too far.

Theo had never brought a woman back to his apartment to sleep. Heather had correctly read this as his way of ensuring that no woman got her foot through the door and started nurturing impossible ideas of permanence. He didn't mind *her* living under the same roof because as far as he was concerned Heather wasn't a threat to his precious independence. She wondered what he would have done had he ever suspected that she was addicted to him. Thrown her out without a backward glance, she imagined.

'Venetia isn't the sort of woman my mother would approve of,' Theo was telling her now, eyebrows raised in amusement at the very thought of it. 'And besides…' He paused thoughtfully. 'I wouldn't like Venetia to think that a brief spell of moving in might lead to something more concrete. With you it would be completely different. You would know the boundaries and wouldn't be stupid enough to think that they could be overstepped.

Anyway—' he shrugged '—my mother's taken to you. She thinks you're very sweet and jolly.'

Heather couldn't think of two adjectives she would have found more insulting, even though she knew that insulting her was the last thing on Theo's mind. He was simply stating a fact.

'Of course I'll compensate you financially for doing this, Heather. Even I realise that it's a favour way beyond the normal call of duty.'

An hour later and Heather was still in a daze at the progression of events. She had moved a select amount of her belongings into his room, choosing to stuff as much as she could into the drawers of the room she currently occupied.

Just standing there, looking around her, made her feel slightly sick. She had always found his bedroom enormous, way too big for one person, with its own small sitting area and a bathroom that could have accommodated a small family. However, with the prospect of sharing it in mind, it suddenly seemed painfully small. Was it her imagination or had the proportions shrunk to the size of a doll's house?

She wouldn't dwell on it, she decided. In a funny way his unconscious insults, the offer of payment, the assumption that she would know her place because she was, after all, no more than a valued housekeeper who happened to be in the wrong place at the wrong time, would strengthen her. He had effectively managed to put her in her place, and as soon as his mother left she would finally have the backbone to walk away.

Having always been a firm believer in the truism that every cloud had a silver lining, Heather now clung to this salutary theory with the tenacity of a drowning man clinging to a lifebelt.

It didn't help that his mother was such a nice person. Over a light supper, she briefly explained to them both what her doctor in Greece had advised, but it was clear that she was much more interested in learning about the new addition to her son's life.

'I have worried about him,' she told Heather in a conspiratorial whisper that was meant to be overheard. 'Too much success with the girls from an early age is not always a good thing for a young boy! It can turn him into a playboy, if that is the correct word!'

Faced with the glorious opportunity to somehow get back at him, Heather smiled and glanced at Theo. He looked uncomfortable and hunted.

'Theo? Oh, no, Theo *would never* see women as playthings—would you?'

The look he shot her from under his lashes was worth every second of the dig, accompanied as it was by a wide-eyed stare of complete innocence. With an inarticulate grunt, he began clearing away the dishes.

'It is very important for a man to settle down,' Litsa was saying, watching approvingly as her son gave off the totally inaccurate impression of someone who habitually helped around the kitchen. 'A good wife is necessary to train a man into being civilised!' She laughed and gave him an affectionate look, while Heather chewed over the ridiculous notion of any woman being able to train Theo Miquel.

'You seem to be flagging, Mama,' he said, shooting Heather a warning glance which she ignored. 'Perhaps it is time for you to retire now. Big day tomorrow. I shall come with you to see the consultant, so you needn't worry yourself unnecessarily.'

He had successfully managed to divert the conversation, but his respite was transitory. Litsa Miquel spent the next forty-five minutes in pleasurable contemplation of her son's settled love life, obviously relieved that she could now share her past concerns about him with someone who understood, and Heather picked up the reins of the conversation with gusto.

It was a unique experience for him to be on the receiving end of female banter that made him squirm, and squirm he did, as childhood escapades were dredged up, until eventually he vaulted to his feet and insisted that he take his mother to her room.

As they disappeared in the direction of the bedroom Heather could feel her ebullient mood evaporating under the weight of reality. Reality was his dismissal of her, made all the more cruel because he wasn't aware of it. It was the bitter emptiness of realising just how far she had sunk in her own estimation—sunk to the level of someone who had been prepared to scramble for the crumbs he had carelessly tossed at her. Reality was the bedroom waiting for her. That thought galvanised her into immediate action. She didn't know how long it would take him to settle his mother, but it wouldn't give her much time to get into her pyjamas and fling herself under the covers, lights off.

For someone who had never seen the allure of strenuous exercise, Heather now discovered that she could move at the speed of light.

She let herself into his bedroom with wings on the soles of her feet and completed her ablutions in five seconds flat. Then, with the door of the bathroom firmly locked, she speedily changed into her pyjamas, which consisted of a pair of small shorts and a vest top. Since she had not heard the sound of a door opening and closing, she assumed he was still with his mother, leaving the coast clear for her to sprint to the bed, leap in, and then switch off the light by the bed.

She dearly wished that she had had the fore-sight to stack some spare linen on the sofa, but there was no way she was going to risk a trip to the laundry cupboard—and anyway he could get it himself. He did precious little around the house as it was, never mind his persuasive acting earlier on when he had strode around the kitchen, tidying up, teacloth draped over one shoulder, for all the world as though he did it on a regular basis.

After one hour of coiled tension, body on red-hot alert for the sound of the door opening, sleep began to take its toll, and by the time Theo did enter the bedroom Heather was sound asleep.

He had been working. His conversation with his mother had been to his mind over-long, despite his fruitless attempts to convince her that she was exhausted and needed to get to sleep immediately. He had never realised just how much she worried about him—about the pressure he was under from work, about his single state. With a fictitious relationship now on the scene, a dam of maternal concerns had been unleashed, and he had left the bedroom feeling slightly battered.

Then had come an awkward conversation with Venetia, as he cancelled plans.

After that, work had seemed to be the only thing, and so he had remained in his office for well over an hour, replying to e-mails that could have easily waited until a more civilised hour.

The sight of Heather in his bed rendered him momentarily disconcerted. She was lying just as she had been months ago, on that sofa, with one arm flung wide. He very much doubted that she had originally lain down in that position of utter abandonment.

Making as little noise as possible, Theo advanced into the bedroom, his eyes getting accustomed to the darkness as he walked tentatively towards the bed, unbuttoning his shirt *en route* before stripping it off and discarding it.

When he had mentioned the sofa, his implication had been that *she* would sleep on it. A faint smile curved the corners of his mouth as he stood over her, watching her as she slept. Fair's fair, he thought wryly. He had twisted her arm to help him out. As far as she was concerned he could take the sofa—or, judging from her deep reluctance to participate in his plan, the floor, and never mind any bedlinen.

He showered quickly, finding himself preoccupied more with the woman lying on his bed and what he would do about her than anything else.

She stirred as he walked back into the room, stark naked. Now he could see the shapely bend of her leg, protruding from under the quilt, and, from the looks of it, whatever she was wearing there wasn't a great deal of it. Was she one of those women who covered themselves up like a nun during the day but then wore sexy little bits of nothing at night? The thought kick-started something in him, some reaction that felt as though it had been waiting there all along for the right time to leap out. He sucked in his breath sharply and turned away, aware of his body's reaction proclaiming a sexual response that was as powerful as it was unexpected.

The sofa, of course, would kill any uninvited thoughts, but he glanced at it, dismissing it as quickly as he saw it.

She was sound asleep, and his bed was infinitely more comfortable than any sofa, especially one that required making up and thus a hunt for bedlinen which would take for ever, considering he had no idea where it was stored.

He soundlessly slipped under the covers and lay down completely still, willing his arousal to subside.

When she restlessly turned over, so that she was now facing in his direction, Theo almost groaned. The small vest left little to the imagination, revealing as it did a generous cleavage which he had never before glimpsed under her daily uniform of baggy tops. His breathing was ragged as he raked her flushed face, her slightly parted lips and the tousle of soft blonde hair framing her face.

He didn't trust himself to look any lower, just in case he lost control.

Lord only knew how long he would have remained there, relishing the pleasurable novelty of wanting a woman with no possibility of having her, if she hadn't stretched—a very small movement that brought her hand into immediate contact with his chest.

He froze as her eyes flew open, and then she shrieked, drawing back from him in horror.

'Keep it down!' he snapped.

'What are you doing here!'

'This is my bedroom, remember? The one you agreed to share?'

'I didn't agree to *share the bed*!' Heather's nervous system was in a state of wild disarray as her eyes locked with his. At the back of her mind, the information was sinking in that he wasn't wearing anything above his waist. What her hand had come into contact with had *not* been the comforting touch of sensible flannelette pyjamas. *Was he wearing anything below*? Her whole body began to burn as her imagination dived off its springboard and took flight.

'The sofa isn't made up,' Theo informed her. Far

from staunching his erection, the shadows and angles of her flustered face were proving an even bigger turn-on.

'Then *go and make it up*! You can't stay in this bed with me! You promised…'

'I never promised anything,' Theo breathed unevenly. 'And stop getting so worked up. It's a big bed.' Which didn't explain why they were lying a matter of ten inches away from one another. He had made no attempt to widen the distance between them. She had certainly tried, but to go any further back would result in her falling off the edge. He could feel her body quivering with tension and ordered himself to get a grip.

'Are you wearing anything?' Heather heard herself stutter, and his silence was telling. 'You're not, are you?'

'I don't possess any pyjamas. I've never seen the point of them.'

'How could you be so…so…*disrespectful?*' Heather whispered, tears gathering at the back of her eyes.

'*Disrespectful?*' Theo was flabbergasted. 'I have no idea what you're talking about.'

'Oh, yes, you do!' Heather said bitterly. 'You're so contemptuous of me that you don't care whether I'm in this bed or not! You don't even care whether you're wearing anything or not! Because as far as you're concerned I might just as well be a…a…*sack of potatoes*!'

In the tense silence that greeted this remark Theo reached out and took her hand.

'Except,' he whispered roughly, 'a sack of potatoes wouldn't have this effect on me!'

Heather felt the hard throb of his erection, and for a few seconds time seemed to stand still. The sexual awareness which had been kept under tabs for so long broke through its flimsy barriers and rushed through her like a tidal wave.

She could hear her own uneven breathing, like someone who has completed a marathon uphill. Every muscle in her body was quivering. He still had his hand covering hers, forcing her to feel for herself the effect of her proximity.

'Well?' he prompted. 'I don't think what you're feeling is the result of a man who is contemptuous of you…'

'You need…need to go and sleep somewhere else…'

'And then pretend in the morning that none of this happened? Why would I do that?' He released her hand, but only so that he could smooth his fingers over her waist, then under the small cropped vest to the bountiful curve of her breast.

Theo groaned. Take away the shapeless garments and she was all woman, all voluptuous, curvy woman, with breasts a man could lose himself in.

With one swift movement he angled his body up so that he was looking down at her.

In the half-light he looked devilishly sexy. His arms were strongly muscled and his beautiful mouth…his beautiful mouth was drawing closer.

With a stifled, hungry gasp, Heather closed her eyes and was lost in his urgent, devouring kiss. With a will of their own her arms curved around his neck, pulling him towards her, and her body writhed, pleading to be stilled.

Eventually, Theo drew back from the kiss— but only so that he could transfer his attention to her neck.

Had he wanted this all along? Had he watched her without even realising it himself? Created fantasies around her? He didn't think so, but if he hadn't why was it now that his body was acting as though attaining the conquest of some private yearning?

He roughly pushed up her vest and then kneeled back on his haunches, the better to appreciate what he had known all along. She wasn't built along the lines of those stick insects he went out with. As a connoisseur of women's bodies, he could say with his hand on his heart that he had never before set eyes on such gloriously abundant breasts. He reached down and felt the weight of them in his hands, and then, very slowly, appreciating every second of the experience, he rubbed the pads of his thumbs over her defined nipples. The tips were hard and he watched, fascinated and unbearably turned on, as she wriggled under his touch, her eyes still firmly closed and her hands balled into fists.

'You have amazing breasts,' he breathed shakily, and her eyes flickered open.

'By that, I take it you mean *big*?' She had never, ever associated the word *big* with anything complimentary, at least not when it came to her body, but the way he was looking at her now was making her feel very sexy, very proud of the breasts she had become accustomed to concealing.

'Amazing,' he corrected. He bent down and tenderly began to suckle on one full nipple, licking and drawing the swollen bud into his mouth until she was moaning with pleasure.

Heather feverishly lifted the vest over her head while he continued his assault on her breasts, dividing his attention between the two until she thought she was literally going to pass out from ecstasy. During those long nights when she had wistfully wondered what it would be like to have him make love to her, see her as a woman instead of someone he had grown accustomed to having around, the way you might grow accustomed to having a pot plant around, during those nights she had never dreamed that the reality would be so exquisitely more fulfilling.

With every fibre of her body she responded to his caress.

She reached to touch him, to feel him, and shuddered with a heady sense of power when he groaned in response.

So this was what it felt like to have this beautiful, wonderful, clever man surrender! To see him shed that formidable control! She arched up and he wrenched the shorts off her, hands hot and urgent.

Heather shifted and felt his hands cover her down there, then his fingers were exploring her telling wetness, rubbing and pressing against the pulsating sensitised bud that sent shock waves of pleasure racing through her.

With a feeling of aching, pounding anticipation, she felt his mouth travel over the flat planes of her stomach—the stomach she had always unfavourably compared to her sister's, the stomach he didn't seem repulsed by—until he was nuzzling into the soft downy hair that veiled her womanhood.

'You can't!' Heather gasped, and he looked up and met her eyes with an amused smile.

'Have you never been touched there before?'

'Not in *that* way!'

'What way?' Her look was a mixture of innocence and excitement, and it slammed straight through him, making his blood boil with desire. For one brief moment Theo wondered where all this suffocating sexual tension was coming from. For a man who prided himself on being an expert lover, a lover who took his time and was a master of finesse, he seemed to have been reduced to a wild animal with only one thought on his mind—possession.

Submitting to primal urges he thought he had

mastered a long time ago, Theo breathed in her erotic, musky smell and tenderly flicked his tongue into her.

It took a superhuman feat of will-power not to rise up and thrust into her. Her wetness was driving him crazy, as was her wanton writhing as he explored her with his mouth. Her soft femininity was slippery, and the sweetest thing he had ever tasted. He knew when she was about to tip over the brink, and before she could do that, he quickly and efficiently took the necessary precautions.

By the time he took her, Heather was well on the way to cresting the peak, and just a few deep thrusts sent her hurtling into a sensory experience that was unique for her. Her whole body shuddered as she surrendered to the waves of pleasure that crashed through her, eventually subsiding into a warm glow of pure contentment.

From restless slumber, she was now fully awake. Actually, her body felt charged in a way it never had before. To think that this beautiful man had brought her to such heights, had sated himself in her, filled her with absolute joy.

She turned to him and sighed. 'That was wonderful.' A tiny frown creased her forehead. 'Was it okay for you? I mean,' she continued anxiously, 'I'm not very experienced…'

'You turn me on just the way you are,' Theo growled, pulling her closer to him and possessively draping one leg over hers.

'Did you mean for this to happen?' Heather asked. 'No, of course you didn't. So why did you make love to me?'

Faced with this direct question, Theo was lost for an answer.

'I mean, was it just because I happened to be in your bed? I know you probably think I'm crazy,' Heather continued, suddenly aware that this might not quite qualify as lazy post coital conversation, 'but I really need to know, Theo.'

'Why? Didn't you enjoy it?' He stroked her hair away from her face, touched by her anxiety.

'I thought it was the most wonderful experience I've ever had,' she answered truthfully, and that was enough to send a charge of pure masculine pride soaring through him.

'The *most* wonderful…?' he teased, smiling when she nodded. 'That puts a lot of pressure on me,' he said gravely.

In a split second Heather realised the error of her ways. She had succumbed to him without so much as a struggle. A few half-hearted protests, but then she had foolishly yielded—of course he would now be looking at the whole situation with a sense of mounting alarm.

Theo did not like women who clung. Nor, she imagined, would he like women who behaved like inexperienced, infatuated adolescents. He would want them cool and carefully controlled. She wondered how to backtrack and, even more importantly, how she could assume the façade of being cool and controlled when she had never been either.

'I'm sorry,' Heather apologised stiffly.

'Why be sorry? We just shared a mind-blowing experience.' And out of nowhere, Theo mused. Which just went to prove the point that around every corner a surprise lay in wait. Who would have thought that the woman whose company he had found utterly relaxing and unthreatening could conceal such depths of fire?

'Which,' he added lazily, 'is why I feel under such pressure. I mean, how am I going to top my first performance?'

Heather felt herself go weak with relief. Why would he say that if his intention was to curse himself for his weakness and chuck her out?

Thoughts of moving on with her independent life flew out of her head faster than water pouring down a plughole. She loved this man. They had made love and it had been, in his very own words, a *mind-blowing* experience. She felt as though she was suddenly walking on the clouds. Giddy with joy, she curled against him.

'You have a very sexy body,' Theo murmured, filling his hand with her lush breast. 'Why do you spend so much time covering it up?'

'You should know, Theo,' Heather said shyly, barely able to believe her ears. 'Aren't you supposed to be a connoisseur of women? I'm not built…well, along the lines of a model, am I?'

Theo didn't answer. He was finding it difficult to remember why he had ever been attracted to his past models. He slid his hand along her side, enjoying the womanly dip of her waist and the full, smooth rise of her hip.

'You don't know what it's like going through your teenage years without the advantages of being thin.' Especially, Heather thought, when you had a sister who looked like hers. 'Boys made snide remarks at school and my girlfriends felt sorry for me. It just wasn't cool to have a figure like mine, so I learned to cover it up.'

For the first time she felt truly proud of her curves, especially when he so blatantly enjoyed them. He pushed her gently onto her back and pleasured himself at her breasts. A man could lose himself in them!

Heather sighed with enjoyment and languorously squirmed under his exploring mouth. The heat that had subsided was building up again, and with a soft moan of anticipation she parted her legs so that he could touch her.

Want, need, love and utter fulfilment bathed her in warm joy, and as she curled her fingers into his hair she gave herself up utterly to the experience.

CHAPTER FIVE

OBSERVING his own situation through detached eyes—something Theo was remarkably good at—he knew that he should be feeling trapped and restless. He was, after all, currently occupying his own private vision of hell. His working hours had been severely curtailed. The past fortnight had seen him first at the hospital, where his mother had been recuperating after heart surgery, and then latterly at his apartment, where he had insisted she remain for at least another couple of weeks, until she was strong enough to venture back to Greece.

She had dutifully grumbled, but had given in without too much persuasion.

Theo suspected that his mother was secretly enjoying the relaxation of being pampered. Heather spent part of her day working on her portfolio, but seemed content to sacrifice the remain-

der to taking his mother for little walks and exper-
imenting with Greek food in the kitchen under
Litsa's eagle-eyed tutelage.

'It helps me,' his mother said tetchily, when he
tried to convince her that she needed to take it
easy. 'And I am not doing the cooking, Theo. Just
supervising. What would you want me to do? Lie
in bed all day like an invalid?'

He had diplomatically refrained from pointing
out that she *was* an invalid, whether she chose to
accept the fact or not.

Litsa had never been one to sit around doing
nothing, and she wasn't about to change the habits
of a lifetime. She was also in her element, bonding
with the woman she imagined to be her future
daughter-in-law—and Theo couldn't blame her.
She had, after all, waited long enough.

The fact that his mother was dealing with an
illusion was something that only impinged
slightly on his conscience. The advantages of the
situation as far as his mother's health was involved
were too self-evident. Her progress, the consultant
had told him a few days earlier, had been really
impressive. Theo didn't think that would have
been the case had she been sitting in his flat from

dawn till dusk on her own, with nothing but her own worries and doubts for company.

No, Heather had been good for her—as had the pleasantly warming thought that she was dealing with her son's significant other.

And at the moment, it happened to suit him as well. Even though the invasion of his working life should have had him fuming.

He snapped shut the lid of his laptop computer and headed for the jacket hanging in the wardrobe of his office.

Jackie, his personal assistant, popped her head around the door and surreptitiously glanced at her watch. She knew that his mother was staying with him, and that there had been a minor medical problem which had been dealt with, but it still shocked her whenever she walked into his office at five-thirty to find him getting ready to go.

'Whatever it is, Jackie,' Theo said, without looking around, 'you'll have to cancel it. I'm on my way out.'

'Yes, but…'

'No buts.' He slipped on his jacket and turned to her. 'After five-thirty I'm off duty, until my mother is on her feet and back in Greece.' He began packing his computer into its leather case. He could use his mother as his excuse for the temporary derailment of his working hours, and, yes, he knew that he had to be there for her, that waltzing in at ridiculous hours, long after she would have retired for the night, just wasn't on, but the prospect of Heather waiting for him back at the apartment was an enticing one.

And why not enjoy the holiday? Theo decided, irritably aware that Jackie was still hovering.

'Why don't you head home as well, Jackie?' he said kindly. 'The reports can wait till tomorrow.'

Jackie grinned at him. She hadn't lasted three years as his PA without having a good sense of humour and an ability to speak her mind in the face of any gathering thunder clouds.

'I think I'll make that remark a special entry in my diary tonight,' she said tartly. 'Considering it's the first time you've ever been known to admit that *anything* can actually wait until tomorrow.'

'Keeping diaries is a very sad hobby for a woman in her forties,' Theo informed her gravely.

'Well, I hope you've managed to keep in *your* diary a certain date for tomorrow evening.'

Theo frowned and opened his mouth to issue an

instruction that all meetings should be off the agenda until he advised otherwise, but Jackie was already continuing in a firm voice, 'It's the annual company do.' She handed him the standard invitation which he had, naturally, committed to memory. 'Everyone will be expecting you to attend.'

Theo knew what the event would be like. His employees would all be waiting to see which bombshell he brought, and far too much alcohol would be consumed, but the food would be good, and as far as morale-boosting went the annual event was always a winner. He would give a short but salutary speech about company profits and bonuses in the pipeline, and would make sure that he stayed for the duration, even though his dates invariably got bored halfway through and began making complaining little noises shortly after dessert was served.

'Wouldn't miss it for the world,' Theo murmured, pocketing the invitation.

'And will you be bringing one of your gorgeous dates?'

'Wait and see, Jackie. Now, clear off. You have diaries to maintain, a husband to feed and children to sort out.'

'I know! Don't I lead a wildly exciting life?'

On the way home, Theo mused on his own less than wildly exciting life. Under normal circumstances he would have left the office no earlier than eight, and would have probably been looking forward to dinner with some extravagantly stunning creature followed by all the sex his heart could desire.

Normal circumstances were lying just round the corner, as far as he was concerned, but in the meantime…

By the time he arrived at the apartment his head was full of images of Heather, who would probably have cooked something and would be waiting for him with his mother, doubtless absorbed in one of those intensely irritating reality shows which seemed to cross all language barriers.

He was whistling as he let himself in.

Heather rose from the chair to greet him, her face wreathed in smiles. 'You mother is much better today, Theo.' She reached up to kiss him, enjoying the lingering feel of his mouth on hers. 'We went for a walk and stopped off at the corner shop to buy some stuff. I've been showing her a typical English meal.' She looked over her shoulder to Litsa, who was smiling at them from the comfort of the sofa. 'Would you like a drink?'

'I'll tell you what I'd like a bit later on, when we're alone.' He brushed his hand casually across her breast and watched her face go bright red.

Heather happily contemplated the night ahead. Life was so wonderful at the moment! A few weeks and whatever rebellious spark she'd had had been extinguished under Theo's lazy caresses at night, his magical, sensitive, amazing lovemaking. She adored his mother, who was brave and wise and gentle…and that said something, didn't it? How many women actually *liked* their boyfriend's mothers?

Because that was what she told herself she was. Theo's girlfriend. And, yes, it had started off as a pretence, but that was then and this was now. And right now she fell into his arms at night, loving every bit of him, and he found her irresistible. He'd told her so himself.

Life couldn't be better!

She had put her career on hold, at least for the moment, and had managed to fob off Beth's exasperation at her lack of direction. The flat, apparently, was still available, but Heather wasn't in the least interested.

She was just too busy enjoying the bliss of living the dream.

When, later, Theo invited her to his company do, Heather closed her eyes with pure happiness and accepted.

Amused at the rapturous expression on her face, Theo felt obliged to tell her that she could expect a very prosaic event. Lots of food and drink and the usual horseplay between the younger members of staff.

Heather barely heard. 'What shall I wear?'

'Go out and buy yourself something,' Theo told her, fast losing interest. He had been looking forward to getting her into bed all evening, and had no intention of wasting time in a pointless female conversation about clothes.

He levered himself up so that he was looking down on her, and really the sight was one he could not get enough of.

He kissed her lingeringly, taking his time. Tonight he would take her to the limits, and then, when she had eventually climbed down, he would carry her there again. He trailed delicate feathery kisses across her neck, and as he bent to lose himself in the wonder of her breasts she tugged him gently by his hair,

'You could come shopping with me…'

'Mmm. Why not?' Theo murmured, breaking his stride to give her one of those ravishing sexy smiles that could turn her limbs to water.

Heather sighed with pure pleasure and gave herself over to enjoying the night.

Theo awoke to find her staring at him intently from the other side of the bed, and he grinned. He had never known a woman so open in her sexual attraction, and it pleased him.

'What time is it?' He flung back the covers and Heather watched, fascinated as always by the sinewy strength of his body. Morning light lovingly showed every flex and movement of his limbs as he slung his legs over the side of the bed before lying back down and pulling her towards him.

'Not quite late enough,' Theo growled, as the covers slipped down, exposing rosy nipples just perfect for sucking.

'Uh-uh.' She primly yanked the covers back up, half tempted to dump the promised shopping expedition in exchange for an hour longer in bed with the man of her dreams. 'Shopping. Remember?'

'Remember what?'

'You said that you would come shopping with me today. I haven't got anything I could possibly wear to a company do, and I'm no good at shopping on my own. I always end up buying the wrong clothes.'

'Did I promise to do that?' Theo frowned, perplexed. 'I honestly don't remember.' He drew back, hating himself for having to dash cold water over her but knowing that taking a day out to shop with a woman, however sexy that woman was, was just a bit too much. 'Well, I'm sorry, Heather. I really can't.'

Heather smiled. At least she tried very hard to. He didn't even remember! He had been so caught up in the business of wanting her that he couldn't even recall something he had said to her, something he had promised. She had gone to sleep wrapped up in the warm, comforting glow of thinking that the following day would bring him out with her, doing something normal couples did, maybe even having lunch out somewhere, and he had gone to sleep, sexually sated and without a thought of her in his head.

'Okay. No problem.' She rolled over, climbed out of bed, and walked self-consciously to the bathroom, her back towards him and tears gathering at a pace in her eyes.

She returned twenty minutes later to find him dressed and waiting for her.

For a heartbeat of a second she hoped that he had had a change of mind, even though she knew that nurturing such a hope was no more than yet another sign of her weakness. Instead he handed her a credit card and told her to go to Harrods, buy whatever she wanted, and put it on his account. He would phone ahead and let them know that she would be coming.

'Right.' Heather took the card, although she had no intention of using it. Hadn't she enough money in her bank account, thanks to him?

'Maybe I can meet you somewhere for lunch,' Theo compromised. For once he was having a struggle with his conscience—although she seemed fine now. He had had an uncomfortable feeling earlier on that she was going to burst into tears, but fortunately he had been mistaken. Tears were not Theo's thing.

'No.' Heather smiled brightly. 'I'll see if I can meet Beth for lunch. I'd like to take your mother, to shop for a few things before she goes back to Greece on Sunday, but I don't think the crowds would do her any good.'

Litsa was going back and Heather wondered what was going to happen to them. Without having to keep up the pretense, would he expect her to return to her jack of all trades status? An hour earlier she would have denied any such possibility, but doubts were beginning to break through the rosy, unrealistic haze of her dreams.

She stood, willing him to try and talk her out of that, but instead he smiled and moved over to her so that he could kiss her on the mouth, and with a pathetic moan of surrender she tugged the lapels of his jacket, pulling him into her.

Satisfied, Theo smiled and wondered where that chill of unease had come from earlier on. He was as safe in the knowledge that she wanted him as much as any man could be safe about anything in this life.

Three hours later Heather left the apartment, and ran full-tilt into the full-blown storm of Beth's misgivings.

'It'll end in tears,' she warned, which was just the thing Heather didn't want to hear. 'If you'd had any sense at all you would never have gone into any ridiculous pretend relationship with the man. He's bad news.'

'It's not a *pretend relationship* now,' Heather defended herself half-heartedly. 'I love him, and I know he feels something for me…'

'Because you were stupid enough to sleep with him?' Beth laughed, but not unkindly. 'Look, Heather, you've got to come back down to Planet Earth and realise that what you have is no more real than any of the other relationships he's had in the past, with all those glamorous women you lost sleep over. Do you remember them? The ones with legs to their armpits and IQs roughly on a par with their ages? Remember them? You should, you know. You bought the goodbye bunches of roses for most of them.'

'Yes, I know, but…' But she was different—wasn't she? She spent nights with him in his bed, in his apartment…she had met his mother…didn't that count for anything? She remembered the way he had dismissed her earlier on, and the burgeoning doubts pushed a little harder against the romantic dreams she had so optimistically and hopefully spun in her head.

'I'm just saying that you've got to be realistic, Heather,' Beth said, determined that she would carry the torch for realism even if her friend was reluctant to. Heather was sweetly and endearingly disingenuous, but Beth had had sufficient experience of men like Theo to know that they could be seriously hazardous to a woman's health.

Beth's version of reality was to drop all stupid notions about for ever after with Theo, and living in his big country house—which, she reminded Heather, she had never been invited to visit—with the happy sounds of kiddies' footsteps clattering across the floors. Reality was to stop spinning fantasies and to start thinking ahead, and the way forward was to include the probability that once Litsa had gone her role with Theo would be effectively over.

'You make him sound like a monster,' Heather cried, appalled because she knew that the man she had fallen in love with could be tremendously funny and thoughtful when he chose to be. She wished that she hadn't bothered to enlist Beth's help in choosing her outfit. She had hoped for some sound advice about colours and styles, maybe a bit of shared excitement that she was going somewhere with Theo—somewhere that involved the people he worked with. She had hoped to find support for her theory that *it meant something*. Instead, she had opened up by confessing that Theo had reneged on his promise to accompany her and it had been downhill ever since.

Beth had taken the afternoon off to help her out, which was very good of her because her lifestyle was frantic, and, having committed to the gesture, she now seemed determined to control the time booked as efficiently as possible.

Heather would have got annoyed, but annoyance was something she only ever attained when pushed to the absolute limit and she knew that her friend was just rooting for her.

So, once lunch and the sermons were over, she greeted the afternoon's shopping spree with a little sigh of resignation.

'First off,' Beth said, after insisting on paying the bill—presumably, Heather thought, in advance sympathy for the chucking out and inevitable poverty which was due to come to her shortly, 'you tell me what sort of clothes you have in mind, and then I'll tell you what I have in mind.'

Heather gave the matter careful thought. A dark colour, she decided, would be right for her figure. Something elegant and straight, so that she didn't stand out. She would be meeting people she didn't know from Adam, and her take on the situation was to blend effortlessly into the background, which she had usually found the safest place to be. She voiced her suggestions hesitantly, making sure to qualify each suggestion with a foolproof reason.

'Wrong, wrong—all wrong,' Beth said with satisfaction, making Heather feel as though she had been unwittingly led into a trap.

Right, right, all right turned out to be a cunning selection of clothes that Heather quailed at the thought of trying on, never mind actually wearing. Shoes would be purchased for style and wow factor, not for comfort. Her hair was going to be tamed, possibly even trimmed, and make-up was going to make a statement—and that statement did not include the concept of looking as though none had been applied. In other words, Heather heard with a sinking heart, a total makeover was on the cards.

'And what's more,' Beth announced, one hand imperiously outstretched to attract a taxi as she looked at her friend over her shoulder, 'you're going to surprise the bastard with this get-up, which means you're going to meet him at the venue. You can change at my place and I'll drop you.'

'Theo's not a bastard.' The rest of the sentence was slowly filtering into her brain with sickening remorselessness.

Beth was on a roll, and once in the taxi she ticked off all the reasons why Heather should follow her lead. She needed to strike out for herself, to prove to Theo that she was her own woman and not the doormat he assumed she was. She needed to break her habit of a lifetime of always, but *always,* dressing down, because the sea was actually teeming with fish—colourful, playful, easygoing fish—and there was no need to get tied up to the biggest shark in town. The day was coming, Beth warned, in the tones of a soothsayer ominously forced to predict the inevitable, when she would be out there on her own, when she could no longer hide away and make do with fairytale dreams. Where would she be if she took flight from reality and cowered inside her flat? Only emerging in clothes that made her invisible? Would she ever be able to find a partner?

Heather was suitably alarmed at the picture painted. 'I don't look good in bright colours,' she ventured. 'And I can't camp out at your place until it's time to go.'

'Why not?'

'Because…' The thought of confidently walking into a venue packed with people she didn't know terrified her. She had managed to live her entire life without ever having to undergo the experience. At least if she arrived with Theo she could hide behind him.

'You'll be fine,' Beth said encouragingly. 'Better than fine. Trust me. Go on. Phone Theo now, before you chicken out.'

Beth's voice was the consistency of honey, and Heather shot her a wry look, but really what she said—*everything* she had said—made sense in a way Heather had always recognised but had never confronted. As soon as she stepped away from her emotional interpretation of the scenario, she could see it for what it was. A pretend relationship that hadn't become real at all. Because Theo hadn't fallen madly in love with her. The pretend relationship had simply become one that involved sex. Apparently, and for reasons she couldn't begin to fathom, he was physically attracted to her. But that meant nothing. As Beth had very kindly pointed out, Theo was attracted to any manner of woman and saw nothing wrong in having sexual relationships that were utterly devoid of significance.

Heather wanted significance. She had been willing to pretend that making love with him was just step one in attaining it. Maybe it was, but probably it wasn't—and anyway, surely it wouldn't be such a bad thing if Theo had a wake-up call? She indulged in the pleasant fantasy of shocking him and realised that Beth had thrust her mobile phone into her hand.

The call to Theo only served to harden her resolve. What had seemed a horrific idea at the time now offered distinct advantages. She was put through to Theo at what was obviously a highly inconvenient time. His voice, when he picked up, was curt. Heather got the feeling that she could have taken a rocket and landed on the moon for all he cared. He was in a meeting, he had no time to talk, and he wasn't about to make time.

'I probably won't be able to get back to the apartment in time to leave with you…'

She could feel herself straining to hear him reject any such thing out of hand, but he didn't. All he said was, *'Fine, you can meet me there. You're a big girl now anyway.'*

A mountain of defeat settled on her shoulders like lead, although she fought to give him the benefit of the doubt in her mind. He was busy. He literally had no time to reassure her or even to chat. And that wasn't his fault. She had hovered around him long enough to know that work was an all-consuming force in his life. She depressed the 'end call' button, blinking away the urge to burst into tears.

'Well?'

'I'm in your hands!'

Beth grinned broadly. 'Good. And don't expect any rest breaks.'

There were none.

Clothes came first. Of course with restrictions on the price, because there was no way that Heather was going to touch the Harrods account card that nestled like a bad omen in her purse. But price restrictions were of no matter to Beth, who confidently declared that youth was all about getting away with wearing cheap because youth could pull it off.

When Heather tried to argue the challenges of her generous figure she was waved down and pulled into shops where clothes of every hue and every cut were tried on and dismissed, or tried on and considered, maybe to return to later.

After dress three, Heather gave up squealing with horror at the amount of flesh being exposed and gave herself over to the experience of being transformed. By outfit six she was beginning to think that she really didn't look too bad with less on. The breasts she had shamefully hidden from the age of thirteen suited the low cut necks of the trendy dresses, and her legs weren't half bad. Yes, her figure was hourglass, but that wasn't necessarily a bad thing. Claire had the model figure, but she had her own physical charm.

She lost count of how many outfits she had tried on before they finally decided on the right one. The fabric was soft and swirly, and clung to her body without cutting into her, and the cut of the dress, with its teasingly daring neckline, revealed a cleavage that most women, Beth assured her, would have died for.

Heather allowed herself to be reassured.

It was also a vibrant turquoise, and against that striking colour her skin looked radiantly healthy and her hair looked more positively fair.

It took less time to find the shoes.

'I'll never be able to actually walk in these,' Heather said, eyeing them sceptically. They were cream and high, and reminded her of the delicate things Claire had used to wear as a teenager—shoes she had always thought she was way too heavy for.

'You don't need to walk. You need to *sashay*.'

Heather decided that sashaying would be just about all she could manage. Hopefully there wouldn't be a fire alarm at any point.

She was beginning to feel transformed already, and, although she wouldn't have dreamt of saying so to Beth, she hoped that Theo would sit up and take notice, maybe have his head turned. She played with the thought as she sat through a stint at the hairdressers, which had been booked earlier in the day.

Her fair hair was dyed to an impossible blonde, although Simon—very camp and very theatrical—

left the rebellious curls, deciding in consultation with Beth that it gave her a provocatively wild look, at odds with her look of wide-eyed innocence.

She laughed when he asked whether she had a brother, but really the makeover had boosted her confidence enormously.

Three hours previously Beth had told her to switch off her mobile phone. Now she itched to switch it back on, so that she could share some of her happiness with Theo. She didn't. She went back to the apartment with Beth, studiously avoiding any talk about the one that was still vacant. That momentary depression had lifted, like clouds on a summer day, and as the time drew nearer not even the tingling of nerves in her stomach could stanch the healthy appreciation of how she looked.

Beth let out a long whistle as Heather stood in front of the full-length mirror and gaped at the stranger staring back at her.

She was striking. The opposite of invisible. Beth had applied her make-up and it was bold without being clownish. Grey eyeshadow, mascara, blusher, lipstick and eyeliner. She looked...*sexy*!

There was a list of *don't*s to accompany the look. *Don't walk fast, don't get drunk, don't talk too much, don't talk too little, don't flirt with the juniors, and, most of all, don't sleep with the boss!*

'This was a good idea,' she confided to Beth, as the car pulled up in front of the hotel. 'I mean, I'm terrified of going in on my own, but…'

'But you need to do that once in a while. It's called independence. Now, *shoo*!'

Heather walked into the hotel, with very small steps for fear of spoiling her new-found image by toppling over on her heels, and discovered for the first time in her life that eyes were swivelling round to look at her.

So this was what it felt like! To walk into a place with your head held high and feel those sidelong interested glances! Instead of shuffling in, hiding behind a group of people, self-consciously aware of your unappealing outfit and hideously aware of what was underneath. Ashamed not to be skinny.

She was shown to the rooms that had been booked for the night, and already crowds were spilling out. A typical office crowd of mixed people, ranging from early twenties to near retirement.

Heather walked in and peered around, and spotted Theo almost immediately. He was standing in a group of people, doing his thing for the younger members of the organisation who were either laughing because they genuinely appreciated his wit or else laughing because they were in the company of the Great Man.

She shimmered through the crowds, noting that the interested glances hadn't stopped, until she was standing directly in Theo's line of vision.

As he registered her presence, Heather gave fulsome thanks to her friend for having ridden roughshod over her wishes and engineered a look that she had tried her hardest to avoid. It was worth every second of those embarrassing moments in dressing rooms, squeezing herself into outfits she would never have considered in a thousand years. Because the way he was looking at her now made it all worthwhile.

Then he was introducing her to the group, moving on to introduce her to fellow directors, and to his personal assistant Jackie, who grinned and whispered to her at some point during the evening, when the drink was beginning to get the better of everyone, that it was such a change to meet one of Theo's dates who actually had something to say for herself.

Heather was in her element. She couldn't remember why she had been so gutted earlier on, because as the evening wore on she could feel his eyes restlessly roving over her, and when, towards the end of the evening, he growled into her ear that if they didn't leave soon he might have to excuse them both to the nearest cloakrooms, so that he could have his wicked way with her, she thought she might die on the spot.

She had obeyed Beth's instructions to the letter, and had made sure not to drink too much, but the little amount of the wine she had imbibed, combined with the fizzing excitement running through her, had put her on a high.

They left towards the very end, after the witching hour. Theo had booked his driver, who was waiting patiently outside.

'You were brilliant,' he murmured, massaging the back of her neck with his thumb. She had been, too. No boredom or whingeing about wanting to leave, no shying away from mixing with his employees from the highest to the lowest.

She had stalked into the room looking magnificent, and he had been impressed and amused to see how she had handled the evening. He also hadn't failed to notice the looks she'd got from some of the guys when they'd thought it was safe to look.

Of course he was comfortably safe in the knowledge that no one would have dared make a pass at her, or even flirt, however tempting she looked. And she certainly *had* looked tempting.

Once in the car, he said something to his driver and slid the dark screen across, enclosing them in a cocoon of privacy.

'So,' Heather said smugly, 'you thought I was *brilliant?* Did the outfit have anything to do with it?'

'You mixed like a trouper,' Theo drawled, pulling her towards him. Not only clothes, but perfume as well. A light, delicate aroma that was subtly tantalising. 'And, yes, the outfit is definitely…' he slid his hand across her waist, curving it up towards the tempting cleavage pouting at him '…very striking indeed…'

Heather shuddered in pleasant expectation of being touched—in the back of a car no less, another first experience for her. He had, he whispered into her ear, as his hand traced the exposed cleft between her breasts, told his driver to take the long route back to his apartment, the *very* long route.

Theo's lovemaking was slow and languorous, though stopping short of full sexual intercourse, which he said would be an uncomfortable shambles because he was simply too big a man to do anything effective in the back of a car, no matter that the car was a big one.

Nor were any clothes shed—which just went to show how erotic touching could be over a forty-five-minute period, at the end of which Heather thought she was going to swoon from being teased with such expertise.

Through the flimsy fabric of her dress he'd managed to send her erogenous zones into hot overdrive. She squirmed, trying to quell the urgent demands her body was making on her, and he continued, ruthlessly turning her on.

It was just as well that Litsa wasn't a particularly light sleeper, and that her room was not too close in proximity to Theo's, because their arrival back at the apartment was a hasty dash towards the bedroom, peeling clothes off along the way, both of them greedy for what had been promised on that very long ride back home.

CHAPTER SIX

HEATHER tried hard to bury the doubts that had sprung up after her shopping trip with Beth. With Litsa ready to leave, they surfaced thick and fast. Just as quickly, she told herself that, yes, she really would address them, but not just yet—not until Theo's mother had left.

She had half hoped that at some point Litsa would decide to tread on unexplored territory and ask Theo what his intentions were, which might have given Heather an opportunity to gauge the ground, but no such luck. Having counted her blessings in seeing her son involved in a relationship with a woman of whom she approved, Litsa was discreet enough not to venture further with her questioning.

And there was no convenient airport wait during which the conversation might have been broached. She was returning to Greece on the family's private jet.

Her heart went out to Theo as he quizzed her on her health, asking her repeatedly whether she wanted to return to Greece, whether it might not be an idea to stay on in London for just a short while longer. But Litsa, like so many older people, missed the familiarity of her normal surroundings. She wanted to return to the peace of the Greek countryside and the routine of friends and old family members.

Theo had arranged for someone to come in daily and take care of her, but he was still worried. Heather wanted to reach out and take his hand, just to give him a bit of reassurance, but she was too uncertain as to how this simple gesture might be greeted.

Which said a lot, she thought. Yet another indication of her doubts, but she succeeded in squashing it.

Hadn't they just spent the most wonderful couple of days? By day, they had capitalised on the few remaining hours of his mother's stay, but the nights had belonged to them, and they'd slaked their passion through into the early hours of the morning.

Now, watching as Theo helped his mother out of the car, Heather attempted to convince herself, yet again, that their soaring passion must surely be a pointer to emotions as yet undisclosed. She smiled brightly at Litsa, pleased that she looked so much better than she had a few weeks ago and sorry that she was leaving.

The hug they gave one another was one of genuine warmth.

'Now, you take good care of my son for me,' Litsa murmured, and Heather's eyes flew to meet Theo's, which were regarding her with some amusement.

'I think it's safe to say that I'm capable of taking care of myself, Mama,' he drawled.

'Every man needs a woman,' Litsa said stoutly, in the tone of someone flatly stating a certainty. 'He may not realise it, but he does. And I am very glad that you have found someone.' Her voice lowered with gentle pleasure.

Heather, watching Theo's face closely, was trying to see how those words were affecting him, but if they were at all then he was keeping it to himself.

'I will be on the phone to you every day, Mama, and don't think that you can tell any untruths about how you are feeling because I will also be on the phone to the nursemaid that I've hired, and to both my uncles.'

'Spied on as though I am not capable of taking care of myself!' Litsa grumbled, allowing herself to be assisted onto the plane. She gave Heather one last backward glance, and they shared a moment of amusement at Theo's authoritarian voice. 'And when will I be seeing you both again?' Litsa demanded. Heather breathed a sigh of relief that some kind of target question had been finally asked.

'Let's jump one hurdle at a time,' Theo murmured. 'Get fully better before you begin issuing invitations.' He broke his non-answer with a smile. 'I have been to enough of your little get-togethers to know that you spend far too much time catering for your guests yourself while your caterers relax with cups of espresso and enjoy the scenery.'

They watched the jet from a distance as it taxied and took flight, and when it finally disappeared into the vast blueness of the sky Heather felt nervous tension swamp her in a way it hadn't done before. She had spent a long time living under the same roof as him, adoring him from a respectable distance, working for him and not

once had she felt this sudden terrifying awareness of his proximity. But, then again, when things
had been on a safe footing she had been able to
exercise a certain control over her emotions.

Even when they had become lovers, thrown into
the same bed by circumstances thrust upon them,
his mother had always been there as an invisible
chaperone against her fragile peace of mind.

No mother now, and no more safety of a relationship that knew its limits. She was in unchar-
ted territory and it scared her to death.

'I hope your mother is all right when she gets
over to Greece,' Heather said, to break the suffocating silence.

Theo, focusing on the road, frowned. 'Why
should she not be?' He glanced over at her. 'I have
arranged everything. She will be met by one of my
uncles and the woman I have employed to look
after her, and there will be no need for her to lift
a finger to do anything.'

'She'll miss having you around, I guess.'

'But she understands that I work here and find
it very difficult to get away for holidays.'

Heather chewed her lip and applied herself to
thinking of something light-hearted she could

say. It was crazy that she had shared so much with him and yet…

The silence between them seemed thunderous. She took a deep breath and began chatting aimlessly about Greece, asking questions about his mother's house and what it was like. When it dawned on her that he might think she was inveigling for an invitation, she branched out, embarrassed, and began to talk about holidays in general.

Meanwhile, under the surface of her chatter, she was aware of the tension building up inside her. She had no idea whether he was feeling the same, but she doubted it. He seemed a little distracted, but that was all, and that was fully explainable considering he had just put his mother on a plane back to Greece and was probably thinking about her, whatever he said about the expertise of his arrangements.

Walking back into the apartment notched up the tension levels substantially higher.

The bedroom they had shared for the past few weeks was just there, to her right. She was aware of it even if she wasn't actually looking at the bed.

Over time, most of her clothes had found their

way into his room—a natural migration because it was so much easier changing there, especially when there was no longer any reason not to. She thought of the intimacy of her toothbrush next to his and felt a little sick at what she knew she had to do.

'Drink?' Theo asked, heading towards the kitchen while Heather trailed along behind him in anxious thoughtful silence.

It was a little after six-thirty. Too early for her to be contemplating wine. But she needed it. She nodded and sat down at the kitchen counter on one of the bar stools.

She waited until he had handed her a glass and then she blurted it out—no preparation, no thinking about how she would phrase what she wanted to say.

'Theo, what happens next?'

Theo paused for the merest breath of a second and looked at her over the rim of his wine glass.

'What do you *want* to happen?' he asked mildly.

Heather met his gorgeous eyes and willed herself not to weaken. 'Your mother's gone now, Theo. There's no need for us to…'

'Carry on being lovers?'

Put like that, their relationship, which meant so

much to her, seemed reduced to the level of two consenting adults sharing a bed for the fun of it. Force of habit and her own upbeat nature immediately kicked in, allowing her to put the most forgiving spin on his baldly enunciated statement. Words of affection did not come easily to a man like Theo. He was depressed, as well, over the whole business with his mother, even though it was something he had not shared with her.

She had to will herself to stop.

'You do me a disservice if you imagine that the only reason I slept with you was to perpetuate a charade for the sake of my mother. You also do yourself a disservice.'

Heather smiled, relieved. 'I'm so glad you said that, Theo. I thought that perhaps…'

'What we have would come to a premature end?' His sexy mouth curved into one of those devastating smiles that could knock her sideways. Heather gulped down a mouthful of wine to steady herself against the temptation to let the conversation go. It was shockingly easy to lose focus when Theo turned on the charm, just like he was doing now, as he strolled towards her, eyes locked into hers, every movement confident of his own massive sex appeal.

Trying to concentrate was like trying to remain upright in a pool of treacle.

He gently removed the wine glass from her hands and leant on the counter separating them so that he could kiss her. This wasn't one of his hot, urgent kisses. There was something touchingly gentle about it, and Heather lost herself in his caressing mouth, distracted for a while from her ground plans.

When he finally drew back her eyes were brimming with compassion.

'I know you were shocked by what happened to your mother, Theo. We never expect any harm to come to our parents, and even when we do we're still never quite ready for it. But she's going to be fine. I know it.'

Coming from anyone else, this expression of sympathy would have been unacceptable and would have immediately frozen his passion, but he looked into her huge blue eyes and was touched by what he saw there.

'I'm so glad I have my very own fortune teller living with me,' he murmured, but not unkindly. 'Would you like to express your sympathy more than just verbally?' He drew back, finished his wine in one long mouthful, and smiled at her with lazy intent.

Heather's determination became a little fuzzy. When he headed towards the bedroom she found that she was following him, as though propelled by legs that had a mind of their own.

'It seems odd…' she said, looking around the bedroom that bore little traces of her everywhere. Her alarm clock, which sat on the table by her side of the bed, the vase of flowers she had put by the window to brighten up the room, the furry bedroom slippers that were tucked under the chair.

'What seems odd?' Theo had moved over to the window to stare outside for a few seconds, before spinning back round to face her.

'Being here without your mother around…'

He laughed. 'Most women might have found it odd the other way around.'

He began stripping off his shirt. Only when he was half naked did he realise that she was still hovering by the door, hands clasped behind her back, when she should have been coming to him, revealing the spectacular body once more hidden under her baggy camouflage clothing.

'Do you want me to do a striptease for you?' he

enquired softly. Thoughts of taking her were releasing him from the coiled tension of seeing his
mother off. He would never have admitted it in so
many words, but he had been worried to death that
she was leaving too soon, that she would have
been better off recuperating in London, where he
could keep an eye on her. He wanted to find sanctuary from his anxious thoughts in the arms of the
woman standing in front of him—a fully clothed
woman who seemed oddly hesitant.

With the superb arrogance of the utterly self-
confident, Theo brushed aside all thought that
Heather might actually not want to hop into bed
with him. His hand hovered over the buckle of his
belt, which he slowly pulled through the loops of
his trousers.

Heather licked her lips nervously. She knew that
if she went any closer to him she would be sucked
in, like a fly getting just a bit too close to the
spider's web. Like a gifted magician, Theo had the
amazing ability to banish thought from her head
and turn her into his obedient puppet.

Heather struggled with the recognition that she
couldn't allow that to happen this time. She had
been gifted a golden opportunity to find out what

she meant to him, whether they could take what they had a stage further now that his mother had gone. She wasn't going to pass the chance up.

'Actually, Theo, I'd quite like just to talk…'

Theo greeted this with narrowed eyes. 'Talk? Talk about what? You've already done the sympathy thing. There's no need to go over old ground. I assure you that I am not about to collapse because I am apprehensive about my mother's health. I will telephone the relevant people on a daily basis, and if I get the slightest whiff of concern then it would be no problem for me to fly to Greece.'

'I'm sure it wouldn't,' Heather said, maintaining her position by the door. It felt safe there. It gave her the illusion that she could do a runner if the conversation got too much for her to handle. 'But actually I wasn't going to talk about your mother.'

'Ah.' Comprehension dawned. 'You want to pick up where we left off earlier on. Is that it? You want my reassurance that I want you, that sleeping with you wasn't just an artificial situation generated by necessity.' He smiled slowly and walked towards her. 'I didn't imagine that I would have to prove my desire to you. You have seen first hand that what you do to my body has nothing to do with make-believe. Oh, no…'

Heather was struggling to breathe. When he was standing right in front of her, she closed her eyes to steady herself. Without the benefit of one lot of senses, she might just be able to control the other four. No good. She might shut him out of her line of vision, but she could still see him in her head. She opened her eyes and took a deep breath.

'I just want to know what happens next…you know…for us…'

Theo wasn't thick. The significance of her words was the verbal equivalent of a very long, very cold shower, or a dip in the North Sea. All traces of passion left his body in a staggering rush, replaced by a cool appraisal of her flushed face.

'I thought you had already asked that question,' he said coolly.

'I know. But you didn't give me an answer.' She risked a quick look at his face and her stomach churned queasily at the expression of icy with-drawal she saw there.

Theo didn't immediately answer. Instead he walked over to where he had dropped his shirt and shrugged it back on. Very good. Half clothed, he was just too distracting. He also remained where he was, by the window, which was very good for her state of mind.

She found that she could actually breathe now.

'Okay.' Theo shrugged. 'The truth is that, yes, we both owe what we have to an unforeseen combination of circumstances. Were it not for my mother arriving, finding you *in situ* and jumping to all the wrong conclusions, then we would never have slept together. However, now that we have, I see no need to disturb the arrangement as it stands.'

Heather was winded, and deeply hurt by his casual assumption that without the intervention of fate in the form of his ill mother he would never have looked at her twice. She had spent almost two years hovering in the background, feeding off the crumbs he had dropped for her, always imagining a day when he would finally see her for the woman that she was. Now she knew that she had been living a dream. She clasped her arms around her and looked down. She was sure the whole world, if it had listened, hard, would have heard the sound of her hammering heart.

Irritated by her continuing silence, Theo frowned. 'Well?' he demanded. 'I might have expected something more by way of response.'

'Something like what, Theo?' All the nebulous feelings she had had since her afternoon with Beth crystallised into a hard knot of miserable re-alization—the sort of miserable realisation that no amount of self-justifying internal clap-trap could cure.

She had waddled around him for years, invisi-ble underneath her camouflage clothing, and then she had somehow landed up naked in his bed. He had happened to like what he had seen, and there-fore had made full use of it.

Moreover, she could hardly blame him when she had been an eager and willing pupil.

'This conversation is beginning to bore me,' Theo announced, strolling out of the room.

Heather, who actually just wanted to find some-where dark and hide away, knew that she couldn't leave things where they lay. Much as she didn't want to follow him, she did—to find him helping himself to something stronger than wine.

'I'm sorry if I'm boring you, Theo. I know you like to keep things superficial with women...'

'There's nothing superficial about sex!' he thundered, banging his glass on the counter with such force that some of its contents splashed and formed a little puddle. He swore silently and grabbed a teatowel, which he proceeded to dump on the spreading patch.

'Well, no…not when it's part of a meaningful relationship…'

He met her eyes steadily. 'Not when it's part of an *enjoyable* relationship. There's the nub, Heather. Relationships can be enjoyable without necessarily being *meaningful*.'

They were both tiptoeing around the central issue. She could either agree with him and back off, take the little he was offering which was a whole lot more than she had ever had in the past, or she could stick to her guns and probably get blown apart in the process.

'I just need to know where we're going, Theo. I mean, is there any kind of future for us?'

Theo, swirling what was left of his drink, could barely believe his ears. He had just offered her something he had never offered another woman before—the chance to have a live-in relationship with him—and what was her response to that?

Questions about longevity, musings about that woolly thing called *a future,* which seemed to occupy women's minds with disproportionate significance.

'I think you've been a little too influenced by my mother.' He poured some of his drink down his throat and then refilled the glass. 'Somewhere along the line you have allowed the myth to become reality. Let me clarify the situation for you, Heather…'

Heather did not want him to clarify the situation for her. Nor did she want to see him looking at her with the cold eyes of a stranger. She wanted him back, the man she loved and knew. But in the space of a second it became perfectly clear that she would never have that man back, because the nature of their relationship had been altered. Like someone trapped on a dizzying, nightmarish rollercoaster ride, Heather felt herself being catapulted towards an inevitable conclusion. There was no getting off the ride now that it had taken off.

Like a rabbit caught in the dazzling headlights of an oncoming car, she stood there, eyes wide, looking at him, half praying that he wouldn't say any more. Her legs felt weak and she sat on a stool, resting her arms on the counter and staring through him and past him.

'Any notion of permanence between us was something created for my mother's benefit. She was weak, and I didn't feel that launching into an explanation of what you were doing living under my roof would have helped her along the road to recovery. She has wanted to see me settled for a long time—too long—and she saw you and flew to the conclusions she wanted to… She still comes from a time when two people living together con-stituted a relationship…'

'We *have* got a relationship, Theo…' Heather wondered whether he could hear the note of pleading in her voice as clearly as she could.

'We have,' he agreed smoothly. 'But one of a purely sexual nature. It's something I hadn't expected, and I'm quite willing for it to continue, but that is all it will ever be.'

'And when will you tell your mother the truth?' Neediness had jumped on her from behind and grabbed her by the throat, and she hated it. Somehow she had waltzed through life without ever really being under the control of anyone or anything. Yes, she had needed to work, but no job had ever meant so much that the thought of losing it had lost her sleep. And, yes, she had friends, and she enjoyed them, but *need*…? No. Now, as she was trampled under the remorseless march of Theo's cool, dispassionate summary of what they had, she could feel her need rising up and making her say things she knew she shouldn't.

'That is something that need not concern you,' Theo answered indifferently. 'When my mother has fully recovered, then I shall tell her that you are no longer a part of my life…that things simply did not work out…we were incompatible…'

Heather nodded dully, fighting back the insane desire to argue her stand, to tell him that they *were* compatible. Hadn't she lived with him for months and months? Hadn't she seen him in his worst lights and his best? Thankfully good sense prevailed and she remained silent.

'She will be disappointed, but she will recover,' Theo continued, with sweeping confidence.

'And will you ever settle down, Theo? Or are there just too many women in the world left to explore?'

Theo didn't care for that at all. Just because he was not ready for commitment it did not mean that he was shallow in his dealings with women. He looked at her through narrowed eyes and told himself that, yes, what was happening was for the best. It had been foolhardy to extend his invitation for them to continue sleeping with one another. Already she was beginning to tap her feet to the invisible sound of wedding bells, and that would never do.

'My life's ambition,' he drawled, with every semblance of boredom, 'is not to sleep with as many women as I can before I die, believe it or not…'

'No, you'll only sleep with them if they can give you a cast-iron guarantee of non-involvement. Not many of those around, Theo.'

Theo was flabbergasted. When had it all changed? If he could have staked money on the one woman who would have been immune to thoughts of marriage, it would have been her. Hadn't she worked for him for nearly two years? Hadn't she seen first hand his views on commitment?

'I cannot believe that you, of all people, can be sitting here and telling me this.'

Since Heather couldn't quite believe it either, she didn't say anything.

'I am not looking for a life partner because at this point in time I need the freedom to pursue my career. I would not be unfair enough to any woman to marry her with the illusion that she would be anything but second place in my life, and what woman would want that?'

Heather almost laughed out loud at that piece of verbal dexterity. So now she was meant to believe that poor Theo was only thinking of the woman—doing her a favour, in fact, by never promising more than what he could deliver that day. And in return all he asked was not to be plagued by anyone being so thoughtless as to suggest that she might be concerned with what happened beyond a twenty-four-hour period!

She wasn't going to have a great long debate with him about that, though. He was as skilful with his words as he was with everything else, and she knew that whatever argument she put forward he would proceed to knock it down, because he wanted to remain in an ivory tower and that was, quite simply, that.

'You're right,' she agreed wearily. 'No woman.'

Theo felt a surge of anger tear through him and fought it down, surprised by his irrational response. He was just doing what he usually did when a woman started fantasising about the impossible. He willed himself to get back in control of his scattered thoughts, and a lifetime of self-discipline came to his rescue.

'Don't you ever get tired, Theo?' Heather asked curiously.

'Tired? Tired of what?'

'Oh, I don't know…tired of the different faces, of playing the field…new dates, new women, new conversation…'

'I thrive on variety.' Theo stood up abruptly and headed towards the sofa. He liked this line of conversation almost as little as he had liked her implication that he was somehow superficial in his dealings with the opposite sex.

That seemed to be a closing statement, and Heather remained on the stool, blinking back her tears. Eventually she stood up and started walking towards the bedroom.

'Reconsidering my offer?' Theo asked casually, and she rounded on him, fury replacing the misery of a few seconds earlier.

'No, *I am not*!' After everything he had said, his arrogance to think that she would even consider some short-lived vacancy as his mistress was just too much. 'I wouldn't *dream* of sleeping in your bed, knowing that at any minute I might be chucked out because you'd got bored and decided it was moving-on time!'

'Then why did you sleep with me in the first place?'

'Your mother assumed…'

'My mother *assumed* that we were in a relationship, which doesn't answer my question… Ah…I see…'

'What do you see…?' Heather blinked in confusion. She had been led into a trap and now he knew what she was all about—knew that she had fallen in love with him. Well, there could be nothing more terrifying for him. Love would have him running that mile even faster than he already was! She had hoped to leave with at least her dignity intact, but now she could see that had been a wild hope.

'I see someone who spotted an opportunity and seized it with both hands.' There was a tone to his voice that Heather had never heard before. It was as flat and as hard as a slab of steel, and she stared at him in speechless bewilderment.

Into the silence, Theo moved onwards, his voice growing colder by the second as he contemplated the full spectre of her deceit. 'I asked myself earlier how things could have changed so drastically between us. For months you were as reliable as the day was long. You took care of the house, you helped me with my work when I needed it, and most of all you never complained. Now here you are, demanding promises of a future…'

'I wasn't *demanding*…I was—'

'*Shut up!*' His voice was like a whip, subduing her into sudden shocked silence once more. In the past, when she had witnessed his anger over something to do with work, he had shown it by stalking round the room, dictating something to her in staccato bursts, his movements restless and fuelled. Now he was perfectly still, and all the more intimidating for that.

'Was it when you supposedly *allowed* yourself to be tempted into bed with me that you started thinking what a good catch I might be? Started thinking that maybe, just maybe, if you played your cards right, you would be in with a chance?'

All colour leached from Heather's face, and her eyes widened in horror at his massive misinterpretation of events.

'Wh-what…?' she stuttered.

'Did you think that if you buttered up my mother you would somehow get one foot over the winning line? After all, you knew that no other woman had ever been in a position to meet any member of my family. Maybe you imagined that circumstances had played right into your hands… You once told me that you believed in fate. Well, what better display of fate than to closet you with my mother for weeks on end?'

'No! None of what you're saying is true!' Heather said, appalled.

Theo, a runaway train gathering momentum, ignored the interruption.

'Sleeping with me, knowing that I lusted after you, must have seemed the icing on the cake!' He thought of the way he had looked forward to stepping through the door, craved the nights when he could make love to her, feel every curve of her body, and he hated himself for the weakness. 'You must have known that I am like any red-blooded male. Throw a naked desirable woman at me and I find it hard to resist.'

With every word he trampled over her fragile hopes, and he was right. She *had* seen his mother's sudden appearance on the scene as a sign of fate. Hadn't she been in the process of really thinking about moving out? And, yes, she *had* hoped that she would come to mean something to him after they had slept together, that he might see her really and truly for the first time. Naïve expectations had found fertile ground in her romantic heart, and time had done the rest.

'When did you first begin to think that I might be worth hunting down? Was it when you first stepped into this place and saw it for the first time?' He remembered her awestruck, wide-eyed pleasure and could have kicked himself for never once thinking that his money might have inspired gold-digging ambitions. At the time he had been amused!

'I don't know how you can sit there and say those things, Theo.'

'Because I am a very practical man. I am also an extremely rich one. And rich, practical men have suspicious minds. You should have taken that into account.'

'This is like a bad dream,' Heather whispered. She felt as though she had been cheerfully living in a house, thinking the walls secure, only to find that the house was made of straw and susceptible to a puff of wind.

'People wake up from bad dreams, Heather. This is no dream. This is reality.'

'Yes. Yes, it is.' And she'd brought it on herself. She blindly turned away, scrambled away from those cold, distant eyes into the bedroom, where she frantically began pulling all her possessions out of drawers, out of cupboards, throwing them on the bed in a heap.

Strains of classical music wafted through the door, a beautiful sound that was incongruous with what she was feeling. Deed done, she assumed that he was now relaxing.

She didn't look in his direction when she walked past towards her old room and the suitcase lying under the bed. She had come with very little and she was leaving with far less. She didn't much care whether her clothes disappeared in a puff of smoke. She hated them, but she made herself pack them. The few that were in her old bedroom and then the rest.

Somewhere along the line he had disappeared, although the CD player was still softly playing Vivaldi. She assumed he would be in the office. Away from her. After so long with him, he was

happy to let her leave his apartment without even
bothering to say goodbye.

In a daze, and with her suitcase, her portfolio
and some assorted bags at her feet, Heather stood
by the front door, not knowing whether to try and
find him or not.

In the end there seemed no point. He had said
what he had to say and he would never believe that
she wasn't an opportunist.

Instead, she hastily scribbled a note, thanking
him for the job he had given her, which had
enabled her to fund her course, and leaving him
the key to his apartment.

From the sanctuary of his office Theo heard the
click of the door being shut, and scowled at the
laptop winking in front of him. She would have
wondered whether to disturb him to say goodbye
and would have hesitated. He knew that because
he seemed to know her so well. Not surprising,
considering they had shared the same space for
such a long time. Big mistake now, in retrospect.

He pushed himself away from the desk and
walked through to the kitchen. Of course this was
the natural and only conclusion. It needn't have
been, if she had agreed to continue their dalli-

ance, but, no, like all women she had wanted him to pay lip service to the non-existent significance of what they had shared. He felt a wall of frustration slam into him. Why she couldn't have accepted what was on offer was a mystery to him, but she hadn't, and so she had to go. He neither needed nor wanted the clutter of a woman in his life—a woman nurturing thoughts of permanence.

Give it a couple of weeks, he told himself, and his head would be clear of her. Until then he would work his guts out and paper over the rough patch with a few dinner dates. Everything back to normal. The way it should be.

CHAPTER SEVEN

SHE had to get out of the flat. Beth had given Heather this piece of advice in a tone of voice that brooked no argument. It had been three weeks, she had pointed out, and three weeks was plenty long enough to pine for a man who had used her.

'I *am* getting out of the flat,' Heather replied, choosing to go with the literal interpretation of her friend's statement. 'I'm toting my portfolio to every publisher and advertising agency in the city. In fact, I'm hardly ever *in*. Actually—' she dangled a carrot tantalisingly in front of Beth, hoping to play the Distraction Card '—I have a second interview with the MacBride agency on Monday. Maybe you could help me shop for a successful interview outfit on the weekend…?'

Beth's response to that was to announce to her friend that she had found her a date. As if, Heather had thought wildly, she was a charitable organisation in need of government aid.

'My counterpart in Dublin, as a matter of fact,' she continued, pleased with herself. 'I've met him a couple of times and he's perfect. Tall, blond, going places…'

Heather would have to wear something stunning, something along the lines of what she had worn for the office party with the GTB, which was Beth's abbreviation for Theo—the Greek Tycoon Bastard. And why not do something with her hair? Some highlights, maybe?

And, as always, Heather found herself half protesting, half glumly acknowledging the sense behind what her friend was saying. And, as always, the half she didn't want to win invariably won.

Which was why she was now, on a Saturday night, standing in front of Beth's floor-to-ceiling mirror in her bedroom, being inspected by her friend like a microbe under a magnifying glass.

And a very satisfying specimen at that, Beth considered with satisfaction. She stood back and gave a low whistle of appreciation. Heather might think that she had been dragged, kicking and screaming, into a date with someone she wasn't interested in meeting, but she needed to get out. Three and a half weeks had seen her drop weight and her normally sunny nature had become worryingly flat. Yes, she had dutifully gone from agency to agency in search of work, just as she had dutifully moved into the vacant flat next to Beth's, and she had obligingly summoned up a pretence of light-heartedness. But underneath she was as empty as a shell.

Whether she appreciated it or not, as far as Beth was concerned, her friend needed to go out and have a good time.

Beth did not believe in letting the grass grow under her feet. Yes, time was a great healer, but with a bit of careful forward planning the healing process could be brought forward in leaps and bounds, and she had approached the problem of her friend with the same logical precision that she applied to her work.

The odd meal out and nights in with girlie chats hadn't worked. Heather had listened whenever Beth broached the subject of Theo, but had stubbornly refused to participate in the cleansing process of conversation. She had listened and resolutely changed the subject.

So step one was to get her friend out in the company of a man. And step two was to show her that there was life beyond Theo Miquel, that he wasn't worth pining over. And what better way to demonstrate that inescapable truth than to manoeuvre her into a position from which she could glean all the evidence with her own eyes?

With breathtaking ease, Beth had arranged the evening out with military precision.

London, for the energetic networker, was a village. It had been relatively easy to find out where Theo Miquel would be on a given Saturday evening. It was prime time and already, with his relationship with Heather not even cold, he was back on the playing field. Beth had even met his latest acquisition—a tall, languid brunette—at a legal do a few months previously, dripping diamonds and hanging on to the arm of one of the law partners in a rival company. Although she wouldn't have dreamt of telling Heather that.

And his weekends with women were not private, romantic one-on-ones for Theo. He would be going to a very expensive, very elite, smoky little jazz club in Notting Hill.

And so would Heather and her hunky dinner date. Beth had arranged it.

'You look wonderful,' she said truthfully. 'Very glamorous. Scott's going to be knocked for six.'

'Is he desperate?' Heather demanded.

'Far from it. He's quite a catch.'

'Then how is it he hasn't been caught yet?' Not that Heather had any intention of catching anyone, but neither was she thrilled to be going out with a rampant serial womaniser just for the sake of it. She thought of Theo, felt her lips wobble and pulled herself together.

'Hasn't found the right woman,' Beth said patiently. 'But he's good company, and a very kind person.'

'Theo could be very kind, you know.'

Beth ignored that. 'The highlights look good on you. Blonde and copper. I'd never have thought of that combination, but it suits you. And your eyes look enormous with that make-up.'

Heather gave herself a desultory glance in the mirror. Three months ago she wouldn't have recognised the woman staring back at her. Gone was the background blob in dark colours with frazzled hair permanently tied up. In its place stood an attractive, now curvaceous woman—thanks to the shedding of nearly half a stone because misery had no appetite. Her outfit was unrevealing, but very clingy. A black dress, pinched in at the waist with a belt, and high black shoes. Beth had lent her a coat, a *faux* fur affair that looked wickedly luxurious.

At her insistence, Scott would be meeting her at the club: some place she had never heard of in Notting Hill, which, aside from the open-air market, was not somewhere she frequented. But she hadn't wanted Scott in her own personal space.

Beth walked her to the door like a clucking, fussy mother hen, leaving her with strict instructions to phone first thing in the morning with an update.

It was a relief to be in the back of a taxi and no longer obliged to try and show excitement. She didn't feel excited. Nothing excited her much nowadays. Not even the prospect of a very good job which she had been given to understand was hers but for the formalities. She thought of Theo constantly, wondering what he was up to and whether he thought of her.

The prospect of spending hours in the company

of someone she didn't know, who would expect her to be brimming over with good cheer, seemed like an exhausting uphill struggle.

It would almost not be such a bad thing if she was stood up. But she arrived to find Scott there, waiting as promised in the outside lobby, and exactly as Beth had described him.

A little over six foot, fair wavy hair, and a warm, pleasant face. He smiled at Heather, and she relaxed and smiled back because there was nothing insolent or threatening in the blue eyes that ran appreciatively over her.

'I thought I might wear a white carnation,' he said, helping her with her coat, 'just in case you missed me. But it seemed a bit corny.'

His voice was as pleasant as his looks, and up close he smelled of some clean, male fragrance.

'Beth gave me quite a detailed description.' Heather smiled again. 'I think she almost wished she'd had a photograph—just in case…'

'I can imagine.' He laughed good-humouredly. 'Beth leaves nothing to chance. It's why she's so good at what she does. Been here before?'

'The club scene's passed me by, I'm afraid…' They had entered the darkly lit cosy confines of a room that curled informally in a U shape around a small stage, in the centre of which a jazz band was playing some whimsical, vaguely familiar tune.

'Tell me about it!'

And, surprisingly, she did. After half a bottle of wine, she even confided her doubts about the evening, and about whether she was ready to start back on the dating scene.

'I'm relieved you said that,' Scott told her, leaning towards her so that he could be heard over the sound of the music, 'because I've just crawled out of a relationship and I'm taking it easy myself. No involvement equals no broken heart.'

'Beth never mentioned it…'

'No?' He laughed and shook his head. 'Clearly taking her matchmaking skills a bit too seriously for her own good.'

'But she means well…'

'And I can't say that I'm having a miserable time. Are you?'

'No.' Heather surprised herself. 'I'm not.'

'Good. Nice to know that I'm not the hard work you expected!' He linked his fingers through hers and gave her hand a friendly squeeze which felt just right, comfortable.

This was just the sort of man she should be falling head over heels with, Heather thought, cupping her face in her hand and thinking about Theo. Someone nice. Someone who was recovering from a broken heart which meant that he had a heart in there somewhere.

She had opened her mouth to share something of what she was thinking with him when she heard the cutting drawl of a familiar voice and her whole body went rigid with shocked awareness.

'Well, well, well…'

Heather twisted round and followed Theo with her eyes until he was standing right in front of them.

She had to blink several times, because it was so surreal seeing him in the flesh. And a few weeks of absence had done nothing to diminish the devastating effect of his sex appeal.

Belatedly she realised that Scott was still clasping her fingers, but when she tried to wriggle free he tightened his grip, before releasing her so that he could stand up and extend his hand in greeting.

It was ignored as Theo glanced away and focused his attention on Heather, who reluctantly stood up and managed a smile.

The palms of her hands felt horrible, sweaty. She pressed them against her sides and widened her smile. 'Theo! What a surprise.'

'Isn't it just?' Theo answered with deadly politeness. 'I had no idea that you came to places like this. I always got the impression that you were content to stay at home, doing your artwork and catching up on TV soaps.'

Heather flushed. If he had intended to make her sound as dull as dishwater, then he had succeeded. Normally slow to anger, she felt a fire begin to burn inside her, and she took a few deep breaths, feeling sorry for Scott—who had been deliberately sidelined by Theo.

'Just the sort of woman I appreciate,' Scott said, joining in the conversation. Although the look he received from Theo was hardly encouraging. 'I'm not much of a club man myself. Much prefer a night in with the television—although documentaries are more my style. Name's Scott, by the way.'

Flustered, Heather completed the introductions, but she was uncomfortably aware that Theo's attention was focused solely on her flaming face.

'It's good to see you, Theo…you're looking well. But I don't want to keep you…'

'You're looking well, too…' His eyes brazenly appraised her with lingering, insolent thoroughness. 'Nice dress.'

'Thank you… Are you here with someone…? Perhaps you should be getting back to your party…' Heather looked around, but the club was dark and crowded.

'Oh, I'm not here with a party…' Theo drawled.

'Right.'

'Michelle's waiting at a table over there, at the back…'

Heather involuntarily followed the direction of his brief nod, and miraculously the crowds seemed to fade into the background—leaving her a clear and unimpeded view of a rake-thin, tall, dark-haired woman sitting on her own, with a flute of champagne in one hand and wearing a scarlet dress that exposed a hell of a lot more than it concealed.

Heather hadn't seriously thought that Theo would spend too long on his own after she had left, but seeing the evidence of just how quickly he had moved on made her stiffen with unaccustomed bitterness.

She suddenly felt deeply grateful that she was

with Scott, and viciously pleased that Theo would see for himself that she, too, wasn't sitting in, counting the seconds go by. Even if that was exactly what she *had* been doing.

'She looks lonely, Theo.' Heather glanced warmly at Scott and then back to Theo. 'I suggest you hurry back to her before someone else comes along and snaps her up. These sorts of places can attract men on the prowl, in case you didn't know.'

'Are you speaking from experience?' He glanced over at Scott questioningly.

'I don't prowl around for women,' Scott said mildly, placing one arm affectionately over Heather's shoulders. 'I'm way too discriminating for that.' He laughed. 'In fact, my friends say I'm too discriminating for my own good. I only settle for…the best…'

Heather flashed him a grateful smile and sank down into her chair, followed by Scott, leaving Theo towering over them both.

Instead of taking the hint and going, though, he leaned forward and planted his hands squarely on the table.

'I myself prefer variety,' he said with a wolfish

smile. 'But each to their own. Now, Heather and I haven't seen each other in a while, so would you mind if I stole her away from you for a dance? I promise to return her to you in one piece.'

'I think we'll let Heather decide whether she wants to dance with you,' Scott said, turning to her.

Theo obviously had a less gentlemanly option in mind, because he didn't give her a chance to voice an opinion. He reached out and clasped her hand in his, and before Heather could protest she was on her feet and being led towards the dance floor, one solicitous hand firmly placed at her elbow.

'How dare you?' Heather whispered, feeling her body react with unwelcome heat to the big, masculine body now pressing uncomfortably close to hers. 'I don't want to dance with you! My date's sitting on his own at the table and it's very rude to abandon him!'

'He didn't seem to mind,' Theo replied dismissively.

He pulled her a little closer. Through the thin little number she was wearing he could feel everything. The thrust of her generous breasts, the small curve of her spine. It enraged him to consider how much he had missed her body. Missed *her.* Although he reasoned that that was just a case of missing a habit. Yes, he had hurled himself back into work, had even made the effort to take Michelle out—a woman he had spoken to for half an hour at a cocktail party the week before and who had emitted all the right signals of being interested. This was his second date with her and she left him cold.

Unlike the small, curvaceous woman now reluctantly dancing with him. He could feel her desire to get away in palpable waves, and wondered whether she was sleeping with the date wilting on his own at her table.

The thought made his teeth snap together in fury.

'So…how are you?' he asked, lowering his voice, perversely desperate to know that she still wanted him.

'You asked me that already.'

'I'm asking you again,' he said irritably.

'Fine. I told you. I'm fine.'

'What have you been up to?' The question emerged in an aggressive, demanding undertone that made her even more tense. He felt it in the way she stiffened in his arms. 'Am I making you nervous?' he asked softly.

Just the sort of sexy voice that had had her head spinning in the past. Did he even *know* that he was doing that? Heather thought of his new conquest, probably seething at the sight of him parading on the dance floor in close proximity with another woman, and a self-protective layer of cold settled over her. She'd never thought that she had it in her to be frosty, but she was fast discovering that she had.

'Don't be ridiculous. Why should you be?'

'You've changed,' Theo said grimly.

'People do.' She shrugged as he spun her around to the melodic tunes of some stupid love song.

'You never used to be so hard,' he said accusingly.

'If by *hard* you mean that I no longer turn to mush whenever you're around, then I'll take that as a compliment.'

'You used to *turn to mush* whenever I was around?' Theo mused with considerable interest. 'I never knew that. For how long?'

'I *meant* that I actually used to…used to…'

'Yes? Carry on. Were you turning to mush before we had a sexual relationship?'

'I'd prefer to forget that!'

'Why would you want to forget something you so obviously enjoyed?'

'This is a ridiculous conversation and I'm not going to carry on with it any more.'

Theo swung her round into a dip that had a few of the other people on the dance floor chuckling with delight, and their eyes locked for a few heart-stopping seconds.

'Why not?' he murmured lazily into her ear, swinging her back into an upright position with an easy flourish. His ego felt gloriously boosted at the thought of the effect he had had on her…for a satisfyingly long time, from the sounds of it. The evening, which had been plodding along, had taken on a wonderful shine.

When the music stopped and she tried to wriggle her way out of his arms he held her tighter.

'I'm sure Stephen—'

'His name's *Scott*!'

'Whatever. I'm sure he won't mind if we have another dance. He doesn't strike me as the sort of fellow to kick up a fuss over something as innocuous as that. Of course he might if he knew our history…'

Heather recognised when she was being played with. She struggled to maintain her composure, and to remember how he had discarded her without a backward glance. He hadn't even bothered to try and get in touch, although he could have. She had told him about the flat opportunity Beth had offered, and he was clever enough to have put two and two together and worked out that she would now be living there. But he hadn't got in touch because he hadn't wanted to. He had picked up the threads of his normal hectic life and hadn't given her a second thought. So much for the sincerity of his well-meaning questions about what she had been up to and how she was! She could be lying under a slab of granite for all he cared!

'We don't *have a history*,' Heather retorted, gaining strength from her thoughts. 'We had a make-believe relationship that lasted a few weeks!' With a little flush of guilt she carried on gently, 'How is your mother anyway? I'm sorry I haven't asked earlier…'

'Getting better and stronger by the day.'

'Have you told her about us?'

'No need to.'

'I did think of her a lot after…after I left, and wondered how she was getting on. She's an amazing woman…so full of enthusiasm and so sharp…sharper than lots of people half her age…'

Theo had no interest in discussing his mother.

'Of course we have a history.' He sidestepped the issue smoothly. 'We didn't just sleep together. We shared a house for well over a year…and I just want to say right now that I apologise for accusing you of targeting me willfully. Like I said, a rich man looks for the hidden agenda when it comes to the fair sex. I had no idea that you wanted me long before we actually ended up in bed together.'

Heather ducked her head. She could feel herself burning up—every part of her. If Scott glanced across at them now he would have to be blind not to realise that this was the man who had made her cautious about the dating scene. Awareness and confusion would be written in blazing symbols on her crimson face.

'Well?' Theo prompted.

'Isn't your girlfriend going to be angry with you for dancing with me?'

'And jealous,' he confirmed, leaning into her so

that his mouth was brushing her ear. 'Especially if she knew what thoughts were going through my head right at this instant. You know, don't you? You can feel what I'm thinking…literally.'

Heather had been so wrapped up in the disastrous twists and turns of their conversation that she had been oblivious to what was now magnificently evident. Theo was in a state of unashamed arousal. She felt immediately faint at the pressure of his hard manhood stirring against her. Her mind, which she had successfully managed to keep under control, sprinted off at a pace and presented her with a graphic, uninvited parade of memories of them in bed together, making love, his big body thrashing above hers. She closed her eyes and had a sickening sense of falling.

'Are *you* jealous?' he whispered into her ear.

'No, of course I'm not,' Heather lied. 'Why should I be? We haven't seen each other for weeks. It's over between us and I'm getting on with life. I have a new flat, a new job and a new boyfriend.' Two out of three wasn't bad—and anyway, technically Scott *was* a boyfriend, if you categorised the term as a friend who happened to be of the male sex.

'How long have you been seeing this Stephen guy?'

'Scott.'

'All of three weeks?'

'That's none of your business, Theo.' Having spent so long sharing her thoughts with him, Heather heard the words leave her mouth and felt a little sense of victory and empowerment.

He might be rampantly turned on by her, but that made him no less of a commitment-phobe than he had been when he had told her to leave. Did he think that he could say whatever he wanted because he thought that she was still the silly fool who had been enraptured by him? Did he think that she hadn't moved on at all?

'I don't think so,' he mused to himself. 'It's not like you to go out hunting for my replacement the day after you leave my apartment.'

You did, she was tempted to retort, but she refused to allow him any insight into how much she was still affected by what had happened. Anyway, concentrating was proving difficult just at the moment.

'So that must mean that he's fresh on the scene. Am I right?' Theo liked the idea of that, because it meant that she wouldn't have slept with the man. Heather just wasn't the type. Heather was… He glanced down at the tight black dress and frowned. Not the sort to wear a dress that managed to cover up all the bits and yet still look provocative at the same time. And not the sort to be coldly giving him the brush-off.

'Have you slept with him?' he asked huskily, and she laughed. *Laughed*! Laughed and refused to answer! 'Answer me!' he growled.

'Why should I answer you? You're no longer a part of my life.' Heather didn't quite know where her strength was coming from. She still loved him, and always would, but those times of mind-lessly allowing him to dictate her behaviour were over—because they had to be. They had slept together and he had still walked away the minute he felt threatened by the possibility of having to give more of himself than he wanted. He hadn't even bothered to try, and she had taken her cue from him.

The jazz number came to a mournful end and they separated. Heather breathed a sigh of relief, because being strong took a lot of energy even if she believed in herself, and Theo breathed hard, disturbed by the gut-wrenching premonition of something slipping away.

'Thanks for the dance,' she said coolly, turning around in mid-sentence to check on Scott, who gave her a little wave which she returned. 'I think you ought to go back to your date now. I can just about see her from here, and she doesn't look very happy.'

Nor did he, come to that. She felt a spurt of female satisfaction. Had he thought that he would run into her accidentally and turn her on with his charm *just because he could*? Did he get turned on by the fact that he felt he could still have her if he wanted, even though there was another woman waiting in the wings? That poor, besotted Heather, who had run around behind him in her dowdy clothes, with her open and trusting nature, was still the same gullible woman he had been forced to turn away because he could smell her becoming a tad too demanding for her own good?

'And yours looks fine,' Theo muttered savagely. 'Wonder what that says?'

'Do you?' She smiled politely at the man who could still make her heart flip, before turning around and walking away, leaving him with her indifference.

Theo quietly seethed for the remainder of the evening. His date was everything a red-blooded male could wish for. Drop-dead gorgeous, attentive, showing green light signals and intellectually unchallenging. No chance of being distracted by serious conversation. Yet he was hugely irritated by her and more irritated by himself as he found his eyes wandering over to where Heather and her bland, blond-haired date seemed to be having a whale of a time. Lots of laughter and body language was speaking volumes.

The minute he saw them rise to leave, he turned to Michelle, cutting her off in mid-sentence.

'We're going.'

She recovered quickly and gave a throaty laugh. 'My place or yours?'

'Yours.' He must really be losing it if he couldn't get worked up about sleeping with this very beddable woman batting her eyelashes at him. 'But sorry, darling. No sex tonight.'

He needed to get back to his apartment and clear his head. Having never suffered the power of jealousy, Theo did not recognise it for what it was. Instead, he directed its force towards himself, ferociously regretting the time he had wasted with that damned woman on his mind. He had had the generosity of nature to actually give her a moment's thought, to wonder what she was up to, when in fact she had being doing very well, thank you very much.

He half heard Michelle's protests as he drove swiftly through the deserted streets of London to drop her off. With his vast experience of women behind him he had no difficulty in recognising the variations in her tone, from understanding to plaintive and finally to apologizing, in case she had done anything to upset the apple cart.

'I'll be in touch,' was all he said when he finally pulled up outside her townhouse. He reached past her to open her door and gritted his teeth when her long fingers gently stroked his forearm.

He was behaving like a cad. That much he knew. He had barely spoken to her for the entire evening, and when he had it had been with a blatant lack of interest.

'I'm sorry, Michelle,' he said, tempering his voice guiltily. 'I haven't been myself tonight. Work, you know.' He let that sweeping generalisation cover over all the cracks and watched her disappointment become tinged with a glimmer of hope. 'And a ton of it to come over the next few weeks,' he added, squashing any temptation she might have to arrange a further meeting. What he needed was a break from the opposite sex. They were trouble.

It was what he continued to tell himself over the next few days as he thundered through his offices, barely aware of his employees scattering like ninepins from his path. Even his secretaries ducked low in an attempt to ride the storm, baffled as to the cause of its eruption.

Finding out Heather's address went some way to defusing Theo's foul temper, but only because he told himself that, whatever lifestyle she had decided to adopt, he was still concerned about her welfare.

Well, he thought, fingering the piece of paper and staring broodingly out of his office window, what reasonable human being wouldn't be?

For all she might be pinning a semblance of sophistication on her shoulders now, Heather was essentially green round the ears—a vulnerable innocent, ripe for being preyed on by anyone with half a brain and an urge to grab what seemed to be on offer. If she had decided to chuck out all her old clothes—*in accordance with the new flat, the new job and the new boyfriend*—and dress with maximum provocation in mind, then God only knew what trouble she was headed for.

He thought of those lush breasts being paraded around London while every man with two eyes stared, and of what Heather, who would naturally be immune to the effect she was having, would do if one of those leering men decided that looking wasn't going to be enough. Scare him off with her streetwise attitude? Hah!

Realising what he had to do was like the parting of dark clouds by a single shot of sunlight.

Four hours later he had pulled up outside the block of apartments. He killed the engine of his car and took a few moments to think.

For fleeting seconds he wondered what the hell he was doing here, especially as it was later than he had planned—after nine. Then he reminded himself where his duty lay. It lay with giving some sensible advice to a woman he knew—had known intimately. Any relationship they had had was now dead and buried, but as a responsible human being he still felt obliged to offer some advice. He was a man of the world—the sort of man, he reflected, proud of his ability to be truthful to himself, who would be one of those drawn to her if he saw her waltzing along the High Street swinging her hips and wearing a top that left little to the imagination.

With a sigh of self-righteousness, he slipped out of the car and bounded up to the front door, pressing the pad with her number.

The apartment block was very modern, but not unattractive. Attempts had been made to intro-duce some greenery around the façade, and he could glimpse shadowy clumps of shrubs and immature trees to one side.

Inside the apartment, Heather heard the buzz of the front doorbell and wondered who on earth it could be. Big advantage to apartment living. There were never any unannounced visitors. She briefly thought of the last unannounced visitor to an apartment, Theo's mother, and squeezed her eyes tightly shut to block out the image.

'Yes?'

'Heather?'

The deep drawl of Theo's voice slammed into Heather like a shock from a live wire. She still hadn't recovered from bumping into him at that club. She felt as though the air had been sucked out of her lungs and she flopped down on the chair.

'Yes?' Her voice was breathless.

'We need to talk.'

'What about?'

'Nothing that can be said down the end of an intercom. Buzz me in.'

She did. Her mind was awash with a thousand things. He had come to see her. She hadn't thought he would, but he had, and it could only mean that meeting her in that club had reminded him of what he had lost. Hadn't he spent ages dancing with her? Willing to leave his date wilting in a distant corner while he whispered into her ear that he was aroused by *her*?

Her fragile mantle of cool, composed self-assurance fell away in a blink.

She heard the knock on her door and her heart sang. When she opened it, she was smiling.

CHAPTER EIGHT

'Hi. What brings you here?' Heather stood aside to let him in. He had come straight from work, but typically he had already loosened his tie and unbuttoned the top button of his white shirt. It was one of his habits, as though the restraints of a suit were unbearable once he had left his office surroundings.

'So this is the new flat,' Theo remarked, positioning himself squarely in the middle of the room and looking around him.

'Do you like it? It's quite small.'

But it was in a good area, and she had worked out that she would just about be able to cover the rent. Decent places were hard to come by in London, and even though it was really more than she could reasonably afford if she were to actually want a life of any sort, Heather had been grateful to Beth for securing it for her and hanging on to it even though the landlord had had innumerable queries.

'I haven't had much chance to do anything with it as yet,' she continued, edging towards him. 'I've hung a couple of my sketches.'

'I recognise them.' They had come off his wall, leaving oblong spaces which got on his nerves more than he might have expected. He had obviously become accustomed to seeing them there—which only proved yet again how dangerous habit could be.

He strode through to the bedroom, peering in, then the bathroom, and finally the kitchen— which was small, but big enough to fit a tiny square table with four chairs pressed into it. There were no signs of male occupation, but then whatever-his-name-was probably hadn't had time to make his presence felt as yet. If, indeed, he intended to. Heather might fancy *him* as commitment-shy, but she was in for a brutal shock if she imagined that he was so different from half the eligible men roaming the streets of London, willing to sleep with any halfway attractive woman who didn't have the ability to say no. Or, in the case of Heather, the ability to spot a cad from a mile off.

He finally concluded his inspection and returned to where Heather was standing by the two-seater sofa. Just as he had thought, her uniform of shapeless tracksuits had been discarded and she was wearing a pair of faded jeans and a small top which couldn't help but draw his eye to her bounteous breasts.

Thank God he was being magnanimous enough to consider helping her, telling her—as the friend he still was, whatever had happened between them—of the dangers of the opposite sex. He felt a zing of pure satisfaction—and why not when he was being as unselfish as was humanly possible?

'Not bad,' Theo conceded, tearing his eyes away from her and focusing instead on the kitchen to the left of her. 'Small, but not the usual dump most single people get shovelled into.'

'I wouldn't stay in a dump,' Heather protested. She thought of the place she had been renting before she had moved in with Theo and flushed. That hadn't been the height of elegance, that was for sure, but time spent in one of the plushest of penthouse apartments had considerably elevated her expectations of living accommodation. 'Well, not now, anyway,' she amended truthfully. 'Would you like something to drink? Tea? Coffee? I don't have any of the fresh stuff, I'm afraid.'

'Have you got anything stronger? Some whisky would be good.'

'You know I don't drink whisky, Theo. Why would I stock it?' He wasn't throwing himself in her arms, declaring himself a fool for not having realised earlier how much he needed her, and she began to have a few healthy doubts about the reason for his presence in her flat. These, though, she decided to keep to herself. Theo was not a man who could be pushed into saying anything he didn't want to say. He obviously had *something* to say—or else why would he be standing in her flat right now?—but he would say whatever it was in good time. Anyway, once she'd removed the burgeoning little worries beginning to niggle, the anticipation of taking up their relationship once more would be worth the wait.

'What about some wine?'

'I think I could do wine. I had a glass yesterday, and the rest is in the fridge.'

She began walking towards the kitchen, leaving Theo to wonder who she had been sharing the wine with. Heather was not the sort of woman who enjoyed drinking by herself. Which meant that she would have been drinking with someone, and the only person who sprang to his suspicious mind was the opportunist date of a few evenings before. He felt his mouth tighten in an instant, glowering hostility, but soothed his distaste by quickly reminding himself of his generous mission tonight.

'Have you eaten?' Heather asked, stretching up to fetch down a couple of wine glasses and looking at him over her shoulder.

'There's no need to put yourself out on my behalf,' Theo said, 'but, no, I haven't. In fact, I've come straight from work.'

'I haven't eaten either.' She smiled, guiltily aware that she shouldn't really be enjoying his company, having him in her flat. Beth would have a thousand fits if she knew. 'Actually, I've spent the day getting my portfolio together in preparation for my new job. They had a look at the interview but I'm going to take it in anyway when I start—just so that my immediate boss knows what I'm capable of. Beth said that's the only thing to do—make them know from the start that I have the potential to get into the area I want. People don't know what you're capable of unless you blow your own trumpet.' She handed him a glass of wine, noticing how he seemed to dwarf the small kitchen even though he had sat down and pushed the chair back as far as he could, so that he could stretch out his long legs.

This gave Theo the leeway he needed to get across his point, but ramming it home wasn't going to do. Heather was obviously very excited about her brand-new life, and slamming into her about its pitfalls would simply get her back up. He decided to let the evening unwind and drop sufficient casual hints that would build up into an insurmountable wall of unavoidable fact. He sipped the wine, watching her as she smiled at him, cheeks attractively pink.

'This Beth character has too much influence over you,' he contented himself by pointing out. 'If you are going to be cooking something for yourself, then I might share it with you. I'm in no rush this evening.'

Heather was dying to ask what had happened to Michelle. Surely if they were an item she would be around on any evening Theo had free?

'Just some pasta actually.'

'Tell me about this job.'

'Do you want some pasta?' It was on the tip of her tongue to offer to cook him something else instead, but good sense held her back from saying it. Yes, he had come to see her, and she was quietly stunned and overjoyed, but it wasn't quite enough to make her forget what a push-over she had been in the past, putting herself out to do whatever he wanted, even if it was a meal at some ungodly hour of the evening after he had worked his usual mammoth hours and still had more to do.

'Why not?'

'Don't let me push you into having it,' Heather said, with an uncustomary surge of rebellion. 'The sauce is just from a tin, and I know you don't like anything from tins.'

Theo frowned. 'Simply because home cooking is a damn sight healthier, not to mention tastier, than anything you can get from a can. Canned foods are loaded with preservatives.'

'And, of course, you've always had the luxury of never having to take the quick and easy way out…' Before she had come along Theo had had the chef from his favourite restaurant prepare food for him which he could freeze and pull out for instant healthy home-cooked food whenever it happened to suit him.

'I didn't come here to have a pointless argument with you over the advantages and disadvantages of processed food,' Theo grated. 'You were going to tell me about your job…?' He stood up to fetch himself another glass of wine and brushed past her, sending little electric currents whizzing through her body.

Distracted by that fleeting physical contact, Heather forgot the question that had risen to her lips—which had concerned his reasons for coming to see her, now that he mentioned it—and found herself chatting to him about the whole nerve-racking interview through to its happy conclusion.

As she chatted she chopped tomatoes, making a small concession to his distaste of anything pre-prepared, which she added to the concoction from the tin. She also shredded and tossed in a few basil leaves from the little plant she had growing on the counter, and crushed some fresh garlic to give it a bit of extra bite.

The end result looked mouthwateringly home-made, and she ladled good amounts for both of them onto some steaming tagliatelle.

'Very healthy,' Theo announced, eyeing her appraisingly. 'Is this a new diet to go with your new life? You've lost weight.'

Heather was proud of the achievement. There was no way she was going to let on that sheer unhappiness had curbed her healthy appetite, and that in the process something weird but wonderful had happened. She had lost some of her cravings for sweet things. Instead, she nodded, and looked at him over the rim of her glass as she swallowed a mouthful of wine.

'I didn't think you'd noticed,' she said, pleased that he had. In those few glorious, heady weeks when they had been together as a couple he had commented often on how much he adored her body, its fullness. 'But I'll never be a stick insect,' she continued. 'I mean, aside from my waist and stomach, everything's pretty much the same as it was before.'

'I'd noticed that as well. Your breasts are still as luscious as ever.'

Heather blushed and told herself not to get her hopes up, not to imagine that the passing compliment was an indication of things to come. But hope sprang inside her like an unchecked river breaking its banks, and it was all she could do not to tremble.

'You don't have to pay me compliments because I've cooked you a meal, Theo. Anyway, you have a girlfriend, and I'm pretty sure she wouldn't be overjoyed to know that you're sitting in my kitchen making flattering noises about my figure.'

'I wouldn't call Michelle a *girlfriend*. She's a woman I took out on a couple of dates and is no more, as a matter of fact.'

'Oh, dear. Did she get a little too possessive for her own good?'

'At the moment I have just a little too much work to devote time and attention to courting a woman,' Theo said smoothly. Dwelling on his love life wasn't part of his agenda, and particularly not when it came close to discussing their relationship or the demise of it. Post-mortems had never been his thing.

Heather shook her head in admonishment. Actually, she found that hard to believe. From what she had seen of Theo over time, pressure of work played almost no part in his ability to wine, dine and bed the fairer sex. It seemed that oodles of charm, looks and money went a long way to success, with or without the availability of free time.

'All work and no play…'

Theo felt his hackles rise, and with his usual rapid leap of logic worked out why. In all the time she had been living with him, dutifully listening and obeying, she had never questioned him in that tone of voice. He was fast realising that she had broken out of the cocoon to which he had become lazily accustomed and was expressing opinions which went way beyond the point of acceptability.

He ignored the flagrant breach of his boundaries and gave her a slow, curious smile.

'More advice from the house of Beth?' he asked mildly, and, as he'd predicted, she went bright red. The cynical words might be there, but the lack of accompanying polish told their own story. He had never met her friend, although he had heard her mentioned frequently in the past—usually in connection with some ridiculous piece of rampant feminism. Now he could clearly see what was happening. Heather was being swept along on a tide of Girl Power that was essentially not her at all.

But swept along she was. Which just proved how gullible she was. It only stiffened his resolve to steer her away from all possible dangers lurking in her path. Who else was going to do it for her? Certainly not her free-thinking friend, who was quite possibly a man-hater.

'She has a lot of experience,' Heather said defensively. 'She comes into contact with all manner of people in the courts of law, and she's naturally developed a hard shell. Basically, she doesn't get taken for a ride.'

'Which is what happened to you?' His annoyance with this absent but influential friend was increasing at a rate of knots.

Heather maintained a stubborn but pointed silence and his face hardened into implacable lines.

'I don't believe anyone held a gun to your head, forcing you to work for me,' he pointed out. '*In fact*, I don't believe there was any necessity for me to offer you that job in the first place. And, having been offered the job—which, incidentally, was quite a generous package…free accommodation in fairly luxurious surroundings…a good pay cheque at the end of the month…a light enough workload to enable you to carry on with your course, unhampered by concerns over time or money—having been offered all that, you always had the right to turn it down.'

If there was one thing Theo knew how to do, it was to win an argument. Before she could defend herself Heather could see the pitfalls of any point of view she might come up with—because the conciseness and clarity of what he was saying was inescapable. She *had* taken up his offer, and chosen to feed her infatuation with him at her own peril.

Just in case she failed to get the message, and infuriated that she might be trying to pin him down as the big, bad wolf in her head—*especially when he had come to see for her own good*—Theo decided to drive home his point.

'When my mother paid us that unexpected visit and jumped to all the wrong conclusions about our perfectly platonic relationship, yes, I admit I asked you to do me the favour of going along with the pretence for the sake of her health. But I didn't force you to climb into bed with me. I never used you, and you were never taken for a ride. We enjoyed what we had and you always knew that I was not the kind of man who wanted to settle down.'

His words drove into her fragile hopes like a hammer obliterating a cardboard box.

'Look, I didn't come here to argue with you.'

Heather stood up abruptly and began clearing the table, waving down his perfunctory offer to help. In a minute she would be able to speak, but right now her mouth felt as though it was stuffed with cotton wool, and there was the sharp, painful pricking of tears behind her eyelids.

She could feel his eyes narrowed on her as she bustled about, with barely enough room to move. Eventually she turned around, propping herself against the sink, and folded her arms.

'No, of course not. And I don't want to argue with you either. It seems a waste of time when we've known each other…well…for a while…' Civilised and mature was how she sounded, which was the only thing Theo could deal with. He certainly wouldn't want her to freak out because she had expected more from this visit than was being extended. Yet again she had misread the circumstances. When was she ever going to learn? Were there courses for people like her? People who allowed their hearts to be eaten up and then dumped all the good advice their friends and their heads gave them so that they could walk right back into the same trap and end up being eaten up all over again?

He still hadn't told her why he *had* come, but she was beginning to think that it was to do with something horribly simple. Like a request for her to come and collect some piece of nonsense she had forgotten at his apartment in her rush to leave.

'Would you like some coffee? I'm afraid I'm going to have to rush you away pretty soon. I'm exhausted.'

'Painting the town red?'

Heather could detect some amusement in his voice, and she pinned a bright smile on.

'Amongst other things,' she said vaguely, stretching the truth like a piece of elastic. 'Now that I've got my own place, I don't see the point of sitting around.'

'More advice from your wise friend?'

'It's very unkind of you to pick holes in Beth when you've never even met her,' Heather felt constrained to point out. She glanced at her watch, then at him.

'Forgot. Exhaustion's kicking in.' He stood up and flexed his muscles. 'Okay. A cup of coffee. I still need to talk to you, and somehow we haven't managed to get around to it.'

'If you want to go and sit down I'll bring you the

coffee.' Knowing that he was in the kitchen, watching her, put her on edge, and right this minute she needed to get her bearings. She needed him out.

She made sure not to make herself any coffee— another hint for him to leave. An image of Beth kept popping into her head, telling her what a good idea it had been to take charge of her life and move out.

She found him sitting on the sofa, leafing through one of her art books, which he proceeded to dump the minute she walked in.

'If you had something to tell me, you could have phoned.' Heather handed him his coffee and retreated to the chair facing him.

She tried to think of him as just an ordinary chap she was no longer involved with. She tried not to absorb the slashing cheekbones, the piercing eyes, the extravagantly handsome features.

'The number here is ex-directory.'

'Oh. Yes.'

'And I couldn't get through on your mobile phone.'

'It broke. I've been meaning to get another one, but I haven't got around to it.'

Theo clicked his tongue in irritation. In this day and age of fast technology Heather was the only person he knew who could blissfully live life without a mobile phone. When she *had* had one, it had generally been left in the house when she was out, or switched off when it was in her bag because she was convinced that it was permanently on the verge of running out of charge. Arguments about the need to have it fully charged and on her person at all times fell on deaf ears, because she was of the opinion that if the world had survived for centuries without its invention, then why should it suddenly be a necessity?

'Please don't lecture me on why I need to go out and buy one tomorrow. I'm quite happy not to have one.'

'What if someone needs to get in touch with you?'

Heather shrugged. 'So why have you come?'

Theo recognised a no-win situation when he heard one, and promptly dropped the contentious matter of the non-existent mobile phone.

'I've come—and I'm not sure how to phrase this—because seeing you in that nightclub with that Sam character…'

'Scott.'

He ignored the interruption. Actually, blessed with almost perfect recall, Theo was well aware of the man's name, but no way was he going to be accurate on the subject and give her any notion that he had been thinking about her and the man in anything more than vague paternalistic terms.

'…made me realise how incurably green around the ears you are.'

'I beg your pardon?' Bewildered, Heather ran her pink tongue over her lips, and Theo's eyes narrowed broodingly.

That, he thought, was a perfect example of what he was talking about. Most women with any nous would know that to be a gesture of pure provocation—but did Heather? Absolutely not. His eyes, which he had obediently kept plastered to her face, now drifted to her breasts, and to the cleavage he couldn't fail to see as she leant forward, all ears.

He felt himself turn on, and lowered his eyes with considerable will-power.

'Look at the way you're sitting.'

More bemused by the second, Heather frowned. It occurred to her to ask whether he had been drinking before he came to visit her, because he wasn't making any sense. Then again, she thought, bringing herself up short, she could hardly trust her own keen sense of deduction, could she?

'How am I sitting? What are you talking about? You haven't come here to talk to me about my posture, have you?' Theo rarely uttered anything that wasn't relevant to what he wanted to say, but she was at a complete loss as to where he was heading with this line of conversation. 'I know I slump,' she said nervously, 'and I'm going to correct that just as soon as I buy my mobile phone.'

He failed to see the limp stab at humour. 'When you lean forward like that, pretty much every-thing is on display.'

Slow colour mounted in Heather's cheeks, and she pushed herself back and fiddled with the neckline of her top. Changing her drab wardrobe in favour of clothes that were younger and fresher had not taken much encouragement on Beth's part. Pleased with her new figure, which for her was probably the slimmest she had been in a very long time, she had enthusiastically taken to the shops and bought herself a range of things that *showed off her assets,* as one of the sales assistants had confidently assured her.

Guilt and a lifetime of circumspection washed over her in a burning tide of embarrassment.

'You don't have to look,' Heather countered belatedly.

'It would be impossible not to.' Theo sat back and linked his fingers on his lap. 'Either you really and truly are not aware of the signals you give off by something as simple as that, or else you are showing me what's on offer deliberately…'

Heather reeled from the humiliating assumption. Theo's ego was big, but she had never known just how big until now. *Did he really think that she was trying to turn him on? That she was desperate enough to do anything to win him back, even after he had reiterated his views to her only minutes earlier?*

Of course he did, she thought in frank, shameful honesty. She had opened that door to him willing to forgive every cutting remark on the simple thread of hope that he had come back with reconciliation in mind. How pathetic was that? Even if he couldn't read her mind, he was astute enough to sense her need, and naturally he would assume, with that splendid arrogance of his, that she would do anything to tempt him back. Including revealing her body.

For a few taut seconds she couldn't think of anything to say, and then she felt a slow rush of anger to her head.

'You really think that I'm sitting here trying to get a response out of you?' she asked, her voice shaking. '*That* is the most arrogant…conceited… *ridiculous* assumption you could *ever* make…'

Theo inclined his head, hearing her out but unmoved by her heated response, and then he shrugged in an exquisitely dismissive gesture.

'That being the case, then you clearly have no idea how to survive in a world that is full of predatory males…'

'Predatory males?' Heather's thoughts stopped on those two simple words and she stared at him, dumbfounded. '*Predatory males*? The world isn't full of predatory males, Theo. Not everyone is built along *your* lines!'

'I am very far from being a predator,' he pointed out with insufferable calm. 'Predators are driven by a need to find and catch their prey. Actually, I have never felt any such need. In fact, I would say that I am more the prey than the predator…'

Heather gasped in disbelief at this wild distortion of fact. 'Are you trying to tell me that you're as innocent as the driven snow?'

'Incorrect analogy. I'm saying no such thing. Merely that women chase *me* more often than not.'

He was probably right too. But that didn't stop him from being an all-time predator of the highest order. Sensing yet another argument she would be in danger of losing, Heather contented herself by fulminating at his high-handed smugness.

'Which brings me to the boyfriend…'

She opened her mouth to refute the label, and closed it as quickly as she had opened it. Scott, actually, had been the sweetest of dates, in so far as they had talked until the early hours of the morning over coffee at her flat. She had listened to him pour his heart out about his ex-girlfriend, on whom he was obviously still hung up, and they had parted company promising to keep in touch.

'Scott isn't a *predator*.' The unlikely thought of that brought a smile to her lips, and seeing it filled

Theo with an uncustomary surge of belligerence which he put down to his unsurprising frustration at her naïveté.

'How would you know? The way you were dressed at that nightclub was a green light to any unattached male. I'm telling you this for your own good, Heather.'

'You came here to *preach to me*? Because you don't think that I'm sensible enough or adult enough to take care of myself?' She stood up, hand outstretched for his cup. 'I think it's time you left, Theo. You should never have come in the first place! What gives you the right to come into my flat and start treating me like a kid?'

'Calm down. You're beginning to sound hysterical.'

Heather laughed hysterically and snatched the coffee from his hands, spilling some on his trousers in the process. Her only regret was that the stuff had gone tepid, although he automatically flinched back and sprang to his feet to brush himself down.

'And I won't be offering to launder them for you!' she shrieked. 'You deserved that!'

Theo, although he didn't show it, was taken

aback by this display of temper. The calm, obliging, sunny-tempered girl… where had she gone?

'For what? For being decent enough to show concern about protecting you?'

Through the red mist of her anger Heather resisted yelling at him that the only person she needed protecting from was *him*—and only because she had been idiotic enough to fall in love with him.

Thinking it managed to bring a few seconds of calm to her shattered thoughts, and she took some deep breaths. When in a crisis, breathe deeply and don't panic. One rule for all situations.

'That's very kind of you,' she managed to say frozenly. 'I do apologise for spilling the coffee on you, but I won't be paying the laundry bill.'

'To hell with the damned trousers!' Theo exploded. He paced the room, finally leaning against the wall and folding his arms. 'I don't care if I have to throw them out! You shriek at me like a *fisherwoman* when *I* am the one who should be aggrieved. You have thrown my good intentions back in my face!'

Heather took a few more deep breaths. So this

was what love did to a person. Turned her from an even-tempered, cheerful sort into a screaming banshee. Her days of mute adoration seemed a lifetime ago—as did tranquillity and peace of mind.

'I can take care of myself.' She folded her arms protectively over her breasts and felt a heady, disturbing rush of awareness as his eyes stripped her of her modest gesture.

'Tip: watch what you wear, and make sure you don't flaunt yourself the way you were doing with me a few moments ago…'

'I'll remember that. Thank you.'

Her sudden compliance got on his nerves and he stared at her narrowly. Maybe—and it wasn't a nice thought—he was trying to lock the gate after the horse had bolted. He suddenly had a driving, obliterating need to find out whether she had slept with her date or not, and there was no way he could reasonably put *that* down to anything caring, concerned or paternalistic.

He walked slowly towards where she was now cringing back into her chair, as if willing the inanimate object to swallow her up, and he leant over her, bracing himself with his hands on either side of her.

Every nerve in her body jumped in wild, searing alarm, and she was aware of her breath coming and going in short, painful bursts.

She kept repeating the mantra about taking deep breaths, but with his face only inches away from hers the exercise was singularly failing to work.

'And did you remember that when you were with your date? Or did you innocently imagine that he was talking to you and not your breasts?'

'Don't you dare insult me like that, Theo.' Her voice lacked conviction, however. She was sickeningly mesmerised by the dark, burning depths of those magnificent eyes.

It *was* an insult, but Theo brazenly outstared her. 'Are you telling me that he didn't manage to get his paws on you?'

'I'm telling you that it's none of your business. Actually, Scott is a really nice guy. He *respects* me—which is more than I can say for you!'

Theo made a sneering sound under his breath and Heather glared at him coldly.

'Scott would never *talk to my breasts*—which is a disgusting expression. I suppose you think that he's wimp, but he isn't. And he would never sneer at me either!'

Thinking back on it, Scott, in an ideal world, would have been the perfect partner. Her eyes misted over at the sheer unfairness of life, and as he watched her expression change some new emotion was added to the boiling pot in Theo's head. He couldn't put his finger on what it was, but he didn't like it.

He was deeply regretting his generous urge to pay her a surprise visit. He should, he told himself fiercely, have let her loose on the London scene and then just waited until she came crawling back to him. Naturally she wouldn't have found him, but she certainly would have learnt her lesson, and sometimes lessons had to be learnt the hard way.

She was still looking at him in that defensive, wary, but ultimately mulish way, and with a soft groan Theo dipped his head and covered her mouth with his. No gentle kiss, this. Urgency and something powerfully elemental pushed her back into the chair.

For a few breathtaking seconds, caught off guard, Heather gave in to the rapturous pleasure only his mouth could give her. She twisted under the pressure of his hot embrace, and as his hand brushed against her breast she felt her nipples harden in response, straining to be touched and caressed. Imagination filled in all the gaps with remorseless speed, reminding her of how exquisitely his hands would move over her body, and how completely his mouth would seductively follow the path, until her whole body was on the brink of orgasm, waiting only for his hard thrusts to bring her to a state of mindless climax.

But hot on the heels of surrender came reality, and she pushed him back with one sharp jolt.

Theo stood up immediately. His erection was like steel. Painful.

'Were you trying to show me first hand what kind of man I should watch out for?' Heather asked shakily. She felt assaulted—and horribly, horribly turned on. How could her body betray her like that? She couldn't meet his eyes. Not when he might see things there that were shameful. Instead, she twined her fingers convulsively together and held her breath.

'Maybe,' he said, turning away, 'I was trying to show you that settling for second best on the rebound from me isn't such a good idea.'

'Maybe,' Heather burst out tremulously, '*I* don't

want to be the one who's *second best*! Maybe I want to be number one with someone—and why not? What's so odd about that?'

For once she entertained the unusual sight of Theo lost for words. Then, without saying a word, he walked away. Out of the room and out of her life for the second time.

It was only when the door slammed shut behind him that Heather finally gave in to the jag of sobbing that had been threatening to come.

CHAPTER NINE

HEATHER was asleep when her telephone rang. It was a rude awakening from the dream she had been having. In her dream she had risen to glittering heights of success with a job that seemed to be un-related to the one she was taking but which paid bucketloads of money. And there was Theo, present at a sparkling social event which she knew was for her—even though in the dream she was standing on the sidelines, watching. He was looking at her in a different way, in a way that signified respect, and she was basking in the glow of appreciation.

She ignored the phone, wanting the dream to go on and on for ever, but she could feel it disappear-ing like mist in the sun as the phone shrilled next to her on the bedside table.

'It's me,' Theo said flatly, stating the obvious. Heather would have recognised his voice if he had been wearing a handkerchief over his mouth.

Disoriented, she sat up and looked at the illuminated hands of the clock on her dressing table. A little after eleven-thirty. He had only been gone for a matter of an hour and a half! Struggling with the shock of hearing his voice, it took her several minutes before she gathered herself together sufficiently to realise that he was saying something to her down the phone.

'How did you get my telephone number?'

'Have you heard a word I just said?' Theo imagined her in a state of drowsiness, hair everywhere, cheeks pink. He looked across the room and grimaced, then turned away from the person who had made herself at home and was staring with great interest around her. 'Look, the telephone number was scrawled next to the telephone on a jotting pad. I made a note of it—and just as well, as it turns out.'

'Do you know what time it is?'

Theo stifled a groan. He had driven back from her flat in the minimum amount of time, only resisting the temptation of heading for the local pub because there had been no convenient parking on the street outside, and had arrived at his apartment in a foul mood which not even the challenges of his latest deal could alleviate. In what had become a disturbingly familiar pattern, he had stared at the columns of information blinking at him and had had to concentrate very hard to bring it all into meaningful focus.

Having lived his whole life at the control panel—a place of pleasing superiority from where he could orchestrate events and determine the ebb and flow of his life, both public and private—Theo had found it nigh on impossible to cope with the lack of control he had felt ever since Heather had walked out of his apartment.

He had spent a good while telling himself that it had been for the best, that Heather's believing the fantasy of their fictitious relationship had been the inevitable start of the whole thing unravelling. The speed at which it had unravelled had taken him by surprise, but he had had no choice but to do what he'd had to do.

That done, he had assumed that his life would effortlessly continue the way it always had, although he had naturally suspected that she might cross his mind off and on.

When he had found himself thinking of her more than he had anticipated, he had told himself that it was because she had been more than his usual fling. After all, hadn't she worked for him, shared his space, for well over a year?

He would, he'd reasoned to himself, have been inhuman to imagine that they could part company without the occasional lingering aftermath.

He had consoled himself with the thought that he was anything but inhuman.

Seeing her with another man had catapulted all reason out of the window. He had reacted with a fury that had left him shaken.

On the drive back from her flat earlier, he had looked at the situation with honesty and had been forced to admit to himself that his pretence of going over to see her so that he could *give a bit of friendly advice because he was such a good person at heart* had been a load of hogwash. He had driven over to see her because he had been jealous—had been driven by some pressing need to discover whether she and the man were serious.

And, judging from the soft expression on her face when his name was mentioned, he had been forced to concede that they were. Or at least had the potential to be.

Her parting shot about not wanting to be *second best* had seemed to him singularly unfair.

When, he had thought with self-righteous fury, had he *ever* treated her as second best?

Just the opposite! He had given more of himself to her than he ever had to any woman before.

He had spent weeks regulating his work life to be around her more. True, the presence of his mother had kind of necessitated that, but the fact remained that he had striven to arrive home early, and had even accompanied her several times to the supermarket—which was virtually unheard of.

How she could then turn the tables on him and try to make him feel bad about himself was sheer female contrariness.

But going through the unblemished fairness of his attitude still hadn't made him feel any better about walking out on her.

The simple truth of the matter was that he missed her. The apartment suddenly seemed empty and forlorn without her presence.

Having arrived at this conclusion, which had taken him down mental highways and byways he had never travelled before, he had finally abandoned his work, stretched, and approached the situation from an utterly pragmatic point of view.

She might be going out with a non-starter of a man—might actually think that that brought certain advantages—but as far as he was concerned that fledgling relationship was simply a technical hitch.

He wanted her back and he would get her back. Simple as that.

Considerably restored by an active workable plan, he had been on the point of going to bed when the doorbell had rung…

Theo brought his attention back to the reason for his phone call.

'I realise it's an unusual time to call, but you have to get over here. Right now.'

'Why? What's the matter?' Suddenly scared by the tension she could detect in his voice, Heather sat up properly and switched on the bedside light, thereby dispelling all possibility of going back to sleep.

'Nothing that can be discussed over the telephone.'

Questions were zooming through her head in their thousands. Theo was not, generally, an unpredictable man. His visit to her earlier in the evening had been unpredictable enough, but this telephone call out of the blue filled her head with all sorts of unpleasant possibilities—including the overriding one that he had somehow had an accident and was possibly in a bad way. Maybe he had already called an ambulance but needed her there for support. Or at least, she thought, checking herself, to look after the apartment while he was in hospital.

She had images of him lying on the ground, his strong body weakened and broken, and she leapt out of bed, clutching the phone to her ear while she flew around the room, yanking open drawers and pulling out clothes.

'Do I need to bring anything?' she asked anxiously.

'Anything like what?'

'I don't know!' She tried to imagine what someone with broken bones might need, and could come up with nothing except an emergency trip to the nearest casualty department. 'There's a first aid kit in the kitchen. In that cupboard under the sink. It's tucked away behind the dishwasher tablets.' To the best of her knowledge he had never opened that particular cupboard.

Theo, taken aback and somewhat puzzled by this could only say mildly, 'Is there? Thanks. That's helpful to know. I'm going to hang up now. Just make sure you get here fast. In fact, get dressed, and while you're getting dressed I'll send my driver over. He'll be with you in twenty minutes. There's not much traffic on the roads at this time of the night.'

'Right.' Before she could ask any more questions she heard the flat dial tone and went into overdrive, flinging on jeans, tee shirt, jumper. No time for make-up or hair. Just sufficient time to wash her face and quickly brush her teeth.

She should really fly over to Beth's, just to let her know that she wouldn't be in her flat overnight, but the prospect of having to cope with the inevitable barrage of stern cross-examining put her off the prospect. She decided that she would phone her friend first thing in the morning.

Theo's driver arrived in under twenty minutes, as predicted. Knowing how much Theo respected his privacy, and taking the lead from the taciturn middle-aged man who politely ushered her into the back seat, Heather felt it best to maintain a discreet silence—although she was itching to ask questions, just in case…

She half expected to arrive and find an ambulance waiting outside, lights flashing, and men racing about with stretchers or whatever they raced about with when carting off someone with injuries. But the apartment block looked remarkably peaceful.

Having left her key behind, it felt odd for her to buzz on the intercom when she had been accustomed to coming and going as she pleased. Theo answered immediately, releasing the door from the phone inside the apartment.

The ride up in the lift took a mere few seconds which felt like years.

It was something of a shock when, after one knock, the door was opened by a Theo who looked remarkably fit and healthy.

Heather released a long sigh of relief and sagged against the doorframe. 'You haven't fallen and broken your bones,' she breathed.

'I beg your pardon?' Theo gave her a perplexed look from under his lashes. She had thrown some clothes on and clearly had no idea how sexy and ruffled she looked.

Having reached his momentous decision to win her back, he knew that he would have to approach her in a different manner. He recognised that he had taken her for granted—hence her unjustified remarks about being second best. It was something he intended to rectify, so he smiled warmly at her and stood aside.

'You're smiling,' Heather said suspiciously, not budging. She longed to fly inside his apartment, which she missed horribly, even though she had told herself a million times that it was far better having her own place, where she could do her own thing without restriction. 'Why are you smiling? I thought…'

'What…?'

She rapidly revised the truth that had been about to emerge. 'That you weren't in a very good mood when you left earlier. I didn't think you ever wanted to set eyes on me again.'

Theo flushed darkly. The way he had stormed out of her flat was not something he especially wanted to remember. It was distinctly un-cool. Fortunately, something else seemed to be playing on her mind and she rounded on him fiercely, stabbing one finger into his chest.

'And there's nothing *wrong* with you!' she couldn't help but hiss.

'Were you hoping that there would be?' Theo asked, frowning.

Released from her state of dread, Heather could feel herself ready to vent eloquently on the object of her misplaced worry.

She caught herself in the nick of time. She had already suffered one episode of misreading a situation and reacting like a fool. She wasn't about to let on to him now the extent to which she had been worried about him. He might suspect that the glorious life of unbridled freedom she was living was anything but. She inhaled deeply.

'I'm not coming inside until you tell me why you had to get me out of bed at an ungodly hour and come round here.'

'It's not the first time I've got you out of bed at an ungodly hour…' To work, yes, when she had been living with him in her role as general factotum, and later, when his mother had been in the apartment recuperating, to make love. His eyes darkened at the sudden memory and a smile of pure sexiness curved his mouth.

Heather steeled herself against the rampant

heavy-lidded provocation of his gaze. 'And that was fine when it just involved a dressing gown and a few paces to the nearest computer.' She looked at him narrowly. 'Please don't tell me that you dragged me all the way here because you need some work doing.'

Much as Theo was enjoying the sight of her, pleasantly at peace with himself for the first time in weeks now that he had resolved to get her back, they could hardly stand at his door talking indefinitely.

'All will be explained once you're inside. In fact…' he paused to step aside and allow her to pass '…I won't actually have to say a word. It will be self-explanatory.'

Intrigued to death, but still suspicious after her foolish mistake in jumping to all the wrong conclusions earlier on, when he had sprung his visit on her, she scuttled past him, taking care not to come into contact with his body even in passing.

'Okay. So what exactly am I supposed to be doing now? It's late, and I'm not in the mood for games.' Heather folded her arms imperiously and stared around her, aware that he was heading towards the kitchen, cool as a cucumber.

'Wait a few minutes. Care for a drink?'

He didn't wait for her to answer. Instead, he poured her a glass of wine and brought it over to where she was still standing, bristling as much as it was possible to bristle without saying anything.

'Come and sit.' He urged her towards the black leather sofa. 'I really am sorry to have disturbed your sleep…' Theo attempted to look contrite, a sentiment that did not sit easily on his face. 'I myself was working when…'

'When…? When what…?'

He didn't answer, because he didn't have to. Heather followed the direction of his gaze, twisting around with her glass in one hand, and her mouth dropped open.

Standing there in all her natural glory was the sister Heather had not clapped eyes on for longer than she cared to remember. Claire had changed surprisingly little, although her hair seemed much blonder than it had years ago.

A smile of pure pleasure illuminated Heather's face, and after the initial shock she stood up, rested her glass gently on the nearest table, and went towards her sister with outstretched arms.

'Claire.' She hugged her, then stood back, then

hugged her again. 'You never said you were coming!'

Claire allowed herself to be hugged and smiled sheepishly. 'Well, I didn't actually make my mind up until recently,' she said, clearing her throat. 'And then I thought I'd just pay you a surprise visit. You've changed.' This time it was she who stood back and surveyed her sister assessingly. 'You've lost weight or something. Remember what a little podge you used to be?'

All at once Heather was catapulted back through time, back to the days when their roles had been clearly defined, with beautiful Claire winning all the physical plaudits. She blushed and nodded.

'If you had given me some advance warning, I would have…made a bed up for you. I don't live here any more, you see. In fact, I now rent a flat of my own, not too far away.'

Claire had already installed herself on the sofa alongside Theo, and was checking out her surroundings with the same assessing eyes that she had used on her sister. 'Shame. This is an amazing place. As I told Theo when I got here.'

Heather blinked and the disturbing image

settled into focus. Her stunning blonde sister, taller, thinner and prettier than she could ever be in a thousand years of changed ward-robes and weight shedding, sitting next to a man whose dark, devilishly sexy good looks were a striking and yet harmonious contrast, if such a thing were possible.

She felt her cheeks grow pink. Jealousy was trying to burrow its way into her, and it was a huge effort not to succumb. As if to add fuel to the fire, Claire turned to Theo, her face wreathed in smiles, and began an extravagant one-woman monologue on the charms of his apartment.

When Claire bothered to make an effort with men, it was always a sight worth seeing. As an adolescent, Heather had looked on in awe whenever her sister had decided that some boy or other was worth making a play for. Out would come the sweetest of smiles, the liveliest of sidelong glances, the most sincere of expressions, and of course Claire was not stupid. She did not simper banalities like a bimbo. She might not have seen the point of exercising her brain over-much, not when her chosen field of work was acting or modelling, but she could still yank it out of cold storage when it suited her. And from the looks of it, it certainly suited her now.

Heather shuffled to a chair and found it hard to get a word in edgewise. Matters weren't helped by the rapt attention Theo seemed to be giving Claire. All ears, and probably eyes too, Heather thought dazedly.

When she finally managed to make her presence felt, Heather asked her why she had suddenly decided to return to England. Was it a holiday? Was she back for good?

But Claire was now exhausted, it seemed. She yawned delicately, covering her mouth with her hand, and then stood up and stretched. It was very graceful. It made Heather think of some kind of choreographed dance movement. The nasty and uncharitable thought flashed through Heather's head that it was contrived and designed to draw Theo's attention to the pert breasts, the slim waist, the flat brown stomach peeping out when she raised her arms.

She squashed the thought and stood up as well. 'Where are your bags?' Knowing her sister, there would be more than one. 'I'll fetch them. I'm sorry. You must be exhausted. We'll go straight back to my place, and of course you're welcome to stay with me for as long as you're over here.' She smiled, but the smile felt forced, and she didn't want to look at Theo just in case she found him staring at her sister. Men always did. It was a natural reaction they just couldn't help. 'It'll be great catching up in the morning, Claire.' There, that was better. Back into her usual appeasing role, always making life easier for her sister. 'You can tell me what you've been up to.'

'Dear Heather.' Claire gave Theo one of her most wide-eyed expressions of girlish camaraderie. 'She's always been such a *carer*. I know I've been horrid—' she turned to her sister with a rueful smile '—hardly ever getting in touch. But I knew you wouldn't mind. I had dreams…' The implication was that Heather was just a little too dull to have dreams.

Heather hoped guiltily that Claire's move home wasn't going to be a permanent one.

'I have dreams too, Claire.' Asserting herself was an uphill struggle. Having always played the same role in her relationship with her sister, it was woefully easy to slip back into it.

'Have you? Well…look, I've just brought a

couple of bags, and to answer your question, yes, I'm planning on making my home in London.'

'That's super.'

'I shall need somewhere to stay until I get a place of my own…'

'You can stay with me as long as you like. Although it *is* a very small flat…'

'Oh, it'll be fun to share! Remember we used to at home, when we were kids?'

Heather remembered a shared room in which ninety per cent had been given over to her sister's possessions while she'd had to make do with compacting everything she owned into the minimum amount of space. She nearly groaned aloud at the prospect of that recurring.

'Unless,' Claire said, sliding her eyes mischievously over to Theo and lowering her voice huskily, 'some dishy chap comes along and rescues poor little me…'

Heather held her breath and waited for the inevitable offer. After all, wasn't there a vacancy for one housekeeper up for grabs? Housekeeper able and willing to offer services beyond the call of duty? And who could resist Claire's charms? She might not have the elongated stick-like beauty of his usual women, but she had a hell of a lot more vivaciousness. And she wouldn't be one to go harping on about commitment and relationships. She enjoyed her freedom as much as Theo did.

Theo couldn't fail to catch the meaningful glitter in Claire's eye. He stood up smoothly, making sure that he didn't reveal in his eyes the depth of distaste that he felt, and nodded in the direction of the bathroom.

'Your sister had a bath when she arrived,' he told Heather. 'You must have things there to collect…?' He spared Claire a glance, noticing the little pout that changed her face from appealing angel to sulky child.

'Heaps. Thanks for reminding me.' She flounced out.

Theo looked at the cute retreating rear thoughtfully, then walked over to Heather and stared down at her.

'I'm sorry Claire interrupted your evening. I didn't get around to dropping her an e-mail to let her know my new address.' In truth, Heather's e-mails to her sister had become few and far between. Claire rarely replied to the ones she sent, and in the end Heather had confined herself to the occasional one, filling her in on superficial bits of information.

Now, of course, she felt horribly guilty. She had to remind herself that they were no longer kids. They were both adults, and Claire had as much responsibility for maintaining their relationship as she had. But lifelong programming had kicked in. Heather felt muddled. Suddenly she wanted her old self back. The big, sack-like clothes she could hide behind. The ungainly body which had never deserved to be put on display.

'Has she always been like that?' Theo asked quietly, wishing that Heather would at least look at him. But she stubbornly stared down at the ground and shrugged.

'Like what?'

He gently placed his finger under her chin and Heather grudgingly met his eyes.

'Asserting her superiority…putting you down… showing no interest in you or what you've been up to. I could go on. She had quite a little chat with me before you came here. Made sure to let me know in not so many words how poor little Heather had been such a sad thing growing up, such a *brick*…always there in the background helping out.'

Heather couldn't actually reply to this because her throat felt thick with tears of humiliation.

'You don't have to feel sorry for me,' she said in a fierce undertone.

'I don't. You feel sorry for yourself.'

Heather recoiled as if she had been struck. How dared he be so accurate in summing her up? Claire would have had loads of stories to tell and, yes, she could just imagine her sister cleverly putting her down. She wondered whether they had both chuckled over her. Had he told her about their brief fling? Had he confided his own amusement and irritation over the way he had managed to ambush her emotions? She hated herself for thinking like that, and in some part of her knew that Theo was not the type of man to behave in such a manner, but she couldn't think straight. She was fifteen again, fat and gauche and watching from the sidelines as her sister flaunted her good looks and tried to give her little pointers on improving her image.

'I do not!' she retorted feebly. 'Anyway, Claire can't help being the person that she is.'

'I saw my bathroom after she'd used it. How are you going to live with all that clutter in your small flat?'

'Is that your way of telling me that you'll do me a favour by letting her move in here with you?' Like a horse without reins, her imagination galloped along at a pace, disregarding the hurdles and bolting towards a conclusion that left her miserable and sickened. She just couldn't *bear* the thought of Theo and her sister...

Whatever answer he had been about to make was interrupted by Claire, who breezed back into the room gaily waving a larger than average holdall which, she informed Heather, was jampacked with all her cosmetics. 'The bags are over there, in the corner. Would you be a darling and bring them for me? I'm so tired I could lie right down on this floor and fall asleep!'

Heather sighed under her breath. She would have to have a long chat with her sister about the impossibility of staying with her for long. There just wasn't going to be the room to house the mountain of things Claire seemed to have brought over with her—and who only knew what else was sailing its way across the Atlantic, destination one minuscule flat that could barely contain the possessions of its one frugal tenant?

'I'll get my driver to take you to your place. Leave the bags. He'll bring them down for you.'

'You have a driver?' Claire's eyes widened as she digested this further piece of information about Theo's financial status.

'He's very, very, *very* rich,' Heather said, with a lack of tact that shocked her—although when she glanced at Theo it was to find that he was smiling with dry amusement.

'Oh, three *verys* might be one too many,' he murmured, wickedly teasing.

Claire, catching an undertone that Heather seemed oblivious to, waded in quickly, making sure that attention was returned to her. 'One can never be too thin or too rich,' she piped up. 'To quote somebody or other.' She grinned flirtatiously at Theo while Heather ostentatiously avoided them both by planting herself firmly at the door, hand on knob, ready to go.

'So I've heard,' Theo said noncommittally. He reached into his pocket for his mobile and had a swift conversation, unnerved by Claire's china-blue eyes narrowly fixed on him. By the door, Heather was standing in a state of such rigid tension that he felt she might crack if he touched her.

'Thanks again,' Heather said as they congregated around her.

Theo deliberately positioned himself so that his back was to Claire and leant over Heather, resting his arm against the doorframe. 'Okay?' he murmured. Having lived his life on one manageable emotional plane, Theo was now resigned to the wild assortment of feelings the woman standing and glaring roused in him. Right now, the urge to protect her was like a physical need. The phoney, altruistic intentions he had piously claimed for warning her away from Scott now crystallised into a very real, pressing desire that she shouldn't be hurt or overwhelmed by her sister.

Unfortunately, he thought, she was hardly going to believe a word he said on the subject, given that he had already used up his ration of so-called concern for her welfare.

'I'll be seeing you,' he promised, and Heather shot him a jaded, disbelieving look.

'Well,' she muttered, 'if you do, it certainly won't be in your office on all fours, cleaning your floor.'

'Are we ready to leave?' Claire said plaintively, and Theo drew back, cursing under his breath.

'My car should be ready. I'll come down with you.'

'No need!' Heather said brightly. 'We sisters just want to catch up on our own now!'

Claire surrendered grudgingly to this suggestion, but rounded on her sister as soon as they were in the lift and heading down.

'God, Heather, you never told me he was drop-dead gorgeous!'

'If you like that sort of look…'

'Well, yes. I know you go for the more boring type, but he's definitely my kind of guy—and *if I'd had any idea what he looked like I'd have worn something a bit better*!'

Heather was still dwelling on the assumption that she could only ever be interested in boring men. Since when had she let her sister get away with thoughts like that? Had she always accepted Claire's sweeping assumptions that she was someone prepared to let life slip by her while she toiled away in the background, doing nothing in particular?

'Wait a minute,' she objected belatedly, as they stepped into the waiting car—Claire's *oohs* and *ahhs* leaving Heather in no doubt that Theo's already magnificent standing had now flown off the scale— 'since when did you think that I only *go for boring men*?' It took a lot of courage to stand up for herself, and she could feel her neck begin to prickle uncomfortably.

She waited for Claire's famous temper to become evident, and was surprised when her sister stared at her, red-faced and open-mouthed. 'I didn't mean that you just *go* for boring guys,' she stuttered. 'It's just that…you know…well…'

'That the only kind of men who would be attracted to me would be the boring type…?'

'You have to admit that dynamic, sexy men would never have given you a second glance in the old days!' Claire burst out, and Heather stared at the stranger sitting next to her coldly. With everything in her she wanted to tell Claire about her fling with Theo, wanted to throw it in her face as proof that she wasn't the eternal no-hoper her sister seemed to think she was. But that would have been a terrible breach of confidence, and since it was apparent that Theo hadn't said a word about it there was no way that she was about to.

'Not that you don't look fantastic now,' Claire conceded. 'In fact I was a little shocked.'

If that was an olive branch, then Heather decided there and then that she would take it. Claire was the only close family member left to her in the world—and anyway, what was the point of bearing a grudge? With her natural inclination to forgive, she told herself that, whatever impression Claire had of her, it had been gained with Heather's assistance. She had meekly lived down to her sister's sweeping generalisations. Even her e-mails had played down her plans for her career. No wonder Claire thought that she had no dreams.

'But getting back to Theo…'

'Must we?'

'Did anything happen between the two of you while you were living in that apartment and working for him?'

Heather frantically tried to come up with a lie that wouldn't be a lie. Eventually she said, with a little self-deprecating laugh, 'I'd be a fool if it had…'

'In which case you wouldn't have a problem if I got in touch with him? You know, just to say thanks for lending me the use of his shower and being so courteous when I showed up at his place out of the blue? Men can be such pigs. Honestly.

Your hair would stand on end if I told you some of the things that have happened to me!'

'Well, no…'

Claire regarded her sister narrowly. 'Good. Because you're way out of his league—and I'm not saying that to be insulting, Heath. Okay, I admit I was out of order to pigeonhole you into the type that old dullards would be attracted to, but…face it… Theo's a sex god, and sex gods just don't look at…well, girls like you…'

'No. No, they don't. They look at girls like you.' And maybe Claire was right. After all, Theo hadn't wanted her in the end, had he? So she had grown in self-confidence. Reality was still a bucket of cold water she couldn't avoid. And, sure, Claire was blunt to the point of rude, but truth was truth, however nicely it was packaged.

For the duration of the trip back Heather was aware from a distance that she was mouthing the right answers as her sister rattled on speculatively about her chances with Theo.

America had taken Claire's arrogance and honed it into a lethal weapon. Heather had visions of Claire gradually dismantling all the confidence she had slowly gathered for herself over time and had to tell herself not to be over-imaginative. But she was finding it difficult to remember the reasons she had once admired her stunning sister, and to put her finger on the loyalty she had always shown to someone who now seemed shallow and just a little cruel.

CHAPTER TEN

HEATHER was standing in the middle of her small sitting area and surveying the sight that now greeted her with dismay.

They had arrived back at the flat the evening before, and after a quick cup of coffee she had retired to bed. That in itself had been a further cause for stress. Claire had objected to being planted on the sofa in the sitting room, claiming that she was so exhausted after her long haul flight that surely she could have the bed for *one night*.

The old Heather would have easily obliged. The new Heather had seen the start of a precedent from which it would be difficult to backtrack. In the complicated world of family dynamics Claire had always been allowed to get her own way, whatever the cost to everyone around her. The bed for 'one night' only would become a permanent state of affairs, and Heather was just not going to let that happen. So she had stuck to her guns and had even refused to make up the sofa, instead handing her disgruntled sister a bundle of linen and, as politely as she could, telling her to get on with it.

Obviously she had got on with more than just making up the sofa and going to sleep. Rudimentary unpacking had begun, and the effects of it were a glaring reminder of why she had to make sure her sister moved out as quickly as possible.

Clothes trailed out of unzipped cases. Some had been stacked on one of the chairs but the rest randomly covered the ground, seemingly in an attempt to stage a complete takeover of all available free space. The towel she had given her sister the night before had been dumped over the coffee table, and the clothes Claire had worn were a rumpled heap at the bottom of the sofa on which she now lay, sleeping like a baby.

Heather's first impulse was to scream. Then to begin tidying up. She did neither. Instead, she marched across to the sofa and gave her sister a brief but very firm shake.

'Come on, Claire. Time to get up.'

'Uh.' Covers were pulled up over her head as Claire squirmed into retreat from the intrusion.

Heather took a deep breath and did the unthinkable. She yanked the covers right off her sister and watched as the very scantily clad body writhed in protest and then Claire finally sat up and glared.

'It's nine,' Heather said calmly. 'And you can't carry on sleeping in here. This place needs to be tidied up, for a start.' She looked around her with irritation. 'I told you last night, Claire, my flat is very small, and I'm not going to live in a state of chaos, cleaning up behind you…'

'I never *asked* you to!'

'Because you assume that I will…!' A flood of unfortunate memories took a stranglehold and Heather had to calm herself by taking deep breaths. Then she perched on the edge of the sofa—the lovely pale sofa she had bought, after much indecision, only a few days previously. 'I'm not tidying up after you, Claire. And I'm not allowing you stay here indefinitely, doing whatever you want to do, bringing back whatever friends you decide to bring back, until such time as something better comes along. This is *my* flat, and you're not going to move in and wreak havoc with it.'

Claire was wide awake now and glaring. 'Mum would have a fit if she could hear you now!'

'That's as maybe…' Heather thought that their mother might have been quite proud. 'But I'm just laying down a few rules and regulations…'

'Oh, you and your rules and regulations!' Claire leapt out of her bed, lean brown body barely clothed in a clinging vest and a pair of stretch pyjama shorts.

Heather noted that her sister was positively bristling with anger, and worked out that for once in her life she was having to deal with the harsh reality of not being treated as special. Claire had done a great deal of bristling in the past, and had always succeeded in getting her own way. Heather thought with some regret of the extent to which she had aided and abetted her sister's selfishness by tiptoeing around her, backing off rather than facing an unpleasant confrontation.

Feeling very serene, she watched as Claire stormed out of the room. There was the sound of the tap being run and things being slammed down in the bathroom, then she was back, scooping up her clothes with the ill grace of a child who had thrown a temper tantrum but lost the battle.

'There,' she announced finally. 'Happy?'

'No. You'll have to clear the lot into your suitcases and then put the suitcases behind the sofa. It's no good piling them into bundles on the ground. There's not enough floor space and it looks horrible.'

While Claire continued to grumble, Heather went and made herself a cup of coffee and some toast for her breakfast. That was something else she wasn't about to start doing. Cooking for her sister, who was faddy in her eating habits and inclined to complain.

No wonder Theo had felt sorry for her, Heather thought sadly. He had sussed Claire out from the word go and presumed that Heather was no match for her.

'You haven't made me any breakfast.' Claire materialised in the doorway of the kitchen and folded her arms. 'If you're going to be horrible to me, then I'll leave right now. I *thought* you might be happy to see me, but *obviously I was wrong.*'

'I *am* happy to see you, Claire, but I'm not so overjoyed that I'm going to hand over the keys to my flat...' *Not to mention my life.* 'Anyway, where would you go?' She sighed. 'I don't understand why you left America in the first place. I thought you were having a brilliant time there. I thought it was the sort of place *where anyone with ambition could strike out.* Not like England which was *too small and narrow-minded.*'

Claire looked uncomfortable, then she shrugged and strolled into the kitchen and began going through the contents of the fridge.

Even from an impersonal point of view, and feeling pretty strong at that moment, Heather could still reluctantly admire her sister's utter contentment with her body. She doubted she would ever get to that point in life, however mentally strong she became. Having always been conditioned to think of herself in elephantine terms, showing off her body would have been an alien concept.

Claire sat on one of the chairs, bread, butter and honey in front of her, and began preparing a sandwich without the benefit of a plate to catch any falling crumbs. Her silky flaxen hair fell around her face like a curtain, flicking up against her thin tanned shoulders. 'Anyway,' she said between mouthfuls, 'I could always go crawling to your pal Theo for a roof over my head.' Her face adopted the expression of someone doing a few mental calculations. 'I mean, I figure he would let me stay, since he knows you and he'd be kind of doing you a favour…'

'You can't do that!' Heather said sharply, her colour rising, and Claire looked at her shrewdly. 'Ah. Why not? Would that be because you don't believe in asking for favours unless you're, like, best friends with someone? Or would it be because you might just be a *teensy-weensy bit jealous*?' She grinned and pretended to look innocently surprised at her own processes of deduction while Heather looked at her in silence. 'I knew it! I just got a *feeling*. I thought that you two might have had something going on, but of course that would have been ridiculous, which means that you must have had some kind of crush on him!'

Heather could feel her sense of power and control begin to seep away. In an effort to hold on to it, she stuck her chin out and said with bravado, 'Why do you assume that Theo and I *didn't* have *something going on,* as you put it?' Phrasing it as a question, Heather didn't feel so bad about revealing the possibility of the truth just to shut her sister up.

With determination, and a good following wind, Claire could strip her of all her defences just when she thought they were firmly in place. Winning the battle over the tidiness issue was one thing, but going back to that place where she had lacked the strength to believe in herself was quite another matter. Heather wasn't about to let that happen without a damn good fight.

'Because I don't. You wouldn't be able to keep that kind of thing to yourself, for a start.'

'I don't want to be having this conversation.' Heather stood up abruptly and turned her back on her sister's amused, taunting face. She felt hot and bothered. In a minute she would have to escape, go out, but she had a sinking feeling that the conversation would resume the minute she was back in her flat. A tide of frustration and anger clawed at her throat. Not only had Theo demolished her life, now here was Claire, picking over the wreckage.

In the midst of her miserable thoughts the doorbell rang, and never had she been more pleased to hear it peal through the flat. She briskly turned around and realised that Claire had similarly risen to her feet. Her privacy was beginning to look like a thing of the past. She didn't stop to question her sister's state of dress. She just felt mightily annoyed at the shadow trailing in her wake as she pulled open the door, expecting to find Beth.

Claire skidded to a halt behind her as Heather stared up at Theo. She was wearing a hunted, harassed expression, and in that fleeting instant Theo knew he had done the right thing. He held out the blood-red roses and stepped through the door, past a shell-shocked Heather, to be confronted by her sister, who seemed to be wearing very little and not be much ashamed of it, judging from the broad smile on her face.

'We were just talking about you,' Claire announced with satisfaction. She strolled across to the sofa and sat down, drawing her knees up. 'That's really sweet of you to bring us some flowers. I love roses. They're my favourite.'

Theo hid the distaste from his face. He couldn't imagine what nature of conversation Heather and her sister had been having, but Heather looked fairly distraught. She had managed to scuttle away, and he could glimpse her in the kitchen, doing something industrious with the roses.

Even with her back to him Theo felt as though

he could read her mood, see it in the slump of her shoulders.

'Come sit by me.' Claire patted a space on the sofa next to her, which Theo ignored. 'I have a little favour to ask of you,' she carried on as Heather emerged from the kitchen, wiping her hands on her trousers and then hovering in the background. Claire obliged him with a hundred-watt smile. 'Heather's been having fits since I arrived here.' She pouted attractively. 'She can't bear the mess—even though I've tidied it all away.' She coiled one strand of that impossibly silky hair around her finger and wriggled her toes. 'So here's my request…is there *any chance* that I might kip down in your place for a couple of days…?' She inclined her head teasingly to one side and managed to give a very good impression of a beautiful lost little kitten in dire need of a kindly helping hand.

Heather gritted her teeth together and wondered what was going through Theo's head. She was only just recovering from the shock of seeing him, and was beginning to wonder about those red roses. He wasn't a flowers and chocolates kind of man. More the sort to get his secretary to purchase something impossibly expensive as a gift, or to arrange a flight to Paris for lunch for a woman. She had done enough gift-purchasing in her time to know that his gestures were expensive but entailed almost no effort on his behalf. She wondered, jealously, if her feisty self-willed sister had managed to strike some chord in him, and was chewing her lip and pondering the possibility when he turned to look at her.

'Somehow I don't think Heather would approve of that arrangement,' Theo drawled, moving behind Heather and resting his hands on her shoulders.

Heather's brain went into immediate shutdown. All she was aware of was the feel of his hands through her top, gently massaging her shoulders, and his warm breath against her hair. Her intention to pull away was brutally ambushed by leaden legs that suddenly couldn't function properly.

Claire's expression had gone from flirtatious helplessness to frank confusion.

'I don't see what Heather has to do with anything,' Claire eventually said, recovering her aplomb. 'Actually, you're wrong about that, anyway. Heather doesn't want me here.' Her lip wobbled. 'She practically told me to leave.'

'I can understand why, judging from the state of chaos in this place.'

'It looks worse than it is,' Claire stammered, backing away at speed from her damsel in distress routine in a scramble to reassure Theo that she would be a very tidy guest. 'I wouldn't make a scrap of mess in your apartment. In fact, I'm kind of looking for work at the moment. I could do whatever Heather did when she worked for you. And...' Claire smiled triumphantly at her sister, unnerved by the way Theo was draped around her protectively '...you wouldn't have to worry that *I* might embarrass you by developing an unhealthy crush...'

Heather wanted the ground to open up and swallow her. Her face had gone bright red. She knew that without the benefit of any mirror. Telling Theo what she had worked out for herself had been a low trick on her sister's part—but then Claire had always been full of low tricks, to which she happily resorted if she thought they would help her get what she wanted. Right now she wanted Theo—and his apartment.

Heather felt movement return to her stricken limbs as Theo moved away from her to stand by the window, obliging Claire to twist around to look at him.

'I don't think you're getting the message, Claire,' he said, his voice dripping cold disdain. 'You won't be staying in my apartment.'

Claire's mouth sagged open in shock, and Heather could see her sister regrouping her ammunition. She almost felt sorry for her. Almost, in fact, waded in with a soothing confirmation of her own offer of free lodging. In the nick of time she bit back the instinctive sympathetic response.

'You haven't told her, have you, darling?'

'Told me *what*?' Claire demanded.

At the same time Heather said, gaping, 'Told her *what*?'

'About us…' Theo felt a powerful kick of sweet satisfaction as he strolled towards Heather. Claire looked as though she had been whacked on the head by a sledgehammer. Her mouth had formed a perfect circle of pure astonishment.

He slung his arm around Heather's shoulder and pulled her against him, expecting some resistance but encountering none. He didn't know why, but his heart was soaring. He could feel her tremble slightly, and he wanted to tip her face up to his and kiss her.

'About *you*?' Claire looked between them in be-wilderment. 'What about you?'

'That we're engaged...'

Heather was appalled by the lie, but just for a few precious moments she savoured the unique sight of her sister looking utterly flabbergasted. The colour had left her face and her attempts to speak emerged as strangled gasps.

Through the fog of her muddled thoughts she was aware of Theo talking, expressing surprise that the little confidence hadn't been shared between sisters—but then they weren't exactly close, were they?

In the middle of his coolly confident revelation Claire leapt to her feet and shot off to the bathroom with a handful of clothes, to re-emerge seconds later, upon which she slammed out of the flat without so much as a goodbye.

Heather felt inclined to say a big thank you to Theo for providing that moment of uncharitable satisfaction—which was wrong, she knew, but she *was* only human after all, and it would do Claire no harm at all to discover that her sister wasn't the complete nitwit she seemed to think she was.

Instead, she wriggled away from Theo and turned to face him, chin up, arms folded.

'What possessed you to say *that*?'

'Are you going to tell me that you didn't get a kick when you saw her face?' In truth, Theo didn't know what had possessed him. Why had he said that? And why did he feel disinclined to *un*say it?

'That's beside the point,' Heather stormed. 'What gives you the right to come here on a *rescue mission*? No, don't interrupt!' She flung herself onto the sofa and hugged one of the cushions to her. Tears squeezed themselves out of the corners of her eyes. 'You felt sorry for me. Am I right? Poor Heather can't look after herself when it comes to the big, wide world. And she can't look after herself when it comes to tackling her sister.'

Theo walked towards her and sat at one end of the sofa, keeping his distance with difficulty.

When there was no reply to her self-pitying outburst she finally looked at him, and looked away just as quickly. Something in his eyes seemed to suck the breath out of her body.

Heather no longer trusted her responses to this man. She reminded herself that in his presence she was continually walking on quicksand. She had given herself wholly to him, and in her naïveté had been pushed away. She wasn't going to repeat the same mistake twice. Although his expression was tearing down her defences and making her want to rush into his arms.

'I can't believe you would enter into this stupid charade all over again,' she said in an unsteady voice.

'That *would* be crazy,' Theo agreed in a low voice.

'Claire isn't going to just disappear conveniently, like your mother did, leaving you the chance to fabricate some story about us drifting apart. She's going to be around, and she's going to be asking loads of questions that I won't be able to answer.'

'I expect she will be.'

Heather looked at him in angry frustration. It was okay for him to sit there, staring at her and agreeing with everything she said, but he wasn't going to have to pick up the pieces. Claire might have been stunned by his revelation, but admitting the truth to her would be equally dramatic. Heather shuddered when she thought about it.

'You have no right to barge into my life and turn it upside down,' she muttered, with heartfelt honesty, and Theo gave her the strangest of looks.

'I might say the same thing about you,' he murmured, flushing darkly.

'I made your life easier.' Heather glared at him over the cushion. 'I was always there, making sure your fridge was stocked and your apartment was clean, buying things for people you didn't have time to buy for, and never complaining when you pointed me in the direction of your computer at ridiculous hours of the night because you had some e-mail or other that just couldn't wait.' She could hear the wobble in her voice as she lashed out at him, but she couldn't seem to help herself any more. Life, recently, had been careering off its tracks, and the arrival of her sister had catapulted it straight off the road.

'You did.'

'And you can stop agreeing with me!' she fumed. 'If you think I'm going to tell you that it was okay for you to concoct a lie about us because Claire was being obnoxious, then you're wrong! *I don't need you to save me*!'

'No, you don't. But maybe I need *you* to save *me*.'

Heather looked at him in sudden confusion. Was this some ploy? Some other remark that she would stupidly proceed to misinterpret, only to repent her mistake afterwards? But his face, as he leaned towards her, was filling her head with a thousand forbidden thoughts and hopes, and her heart was fluttering wildly inside her.

'Don't,' she said abruptly, slipping off the sofa and retreating to the window, where she stood and watched him guardedly from a safe distance.

'Don't what?'

'Trick me with words.'

In mesmerised fascination she watched as he proceeded to follow her, until he was standing right in front of her, then he leant against the wall and stared down at her. 'Tricking you is the one thing I never intended to do,' he murmured roughly. 'If you think that's what I did, then I apologise.'

'You *apologise*?' She looked at him in confusion. 'You never apologise, Theo.'

'The fact is,' he said heavily, 'the only person I managed to trick was myself.' He couldn't help his hand reaching into her hair, smoothing it away from her face, or his thumb caressing her temple. 'We shared the same space, and I kidded myself that the reason I started looking forward to returning to my apartment had nothing to do with the fact that I would find you there. Then we slept together, and I told myself that it was just sex, that there was nothing more involved. When you left I did my damnedest to accept the obvious truth, which was that that was the way it should be because my life had no room for anything more than passing relationships that wouldn't interrupt the big picture. What I didn't realise was that the big picture was all about *you*.'

'What are you saying?' Heather did her best to choke back the flood of hope. She closed her eyes briefly, wishing for this moment to never end.

'You know what I'm saying. I came here to win you back. But I want more than that. I don't just want you back in my apartment, or back in my bed on a temporary basis. I want you in my life for ever.'

'*For ever*?'

'Isn't that what you want too?' He smiled slowly at her, and Heather felt happiness swirl through her from the tips of her toes to the top of her head.

'Yes, I love you. I've always known that.'

'And I love you too. But, fool that I am, I've only just realised it.'

Heather's eyes rounded.

'I hadn't planned on telling your sister that we were engaged, but the minute I said it, it was like *wham*! Everything slotted into place. And I knew that being engaged to you, being married to you, spending the rest of my life with you, was exactly what I wanted. And you *love* me.' He murmured that with considerable masculine satisfaction. 'So will you marry me…?'

Theo did not waste any time. Within four weeks—the most joyful four weeks Heather could ever have envisaged—arrangements were made and they were married in Greece, surrounded by family and friends and fussed over by his mother.

Claire was invited, and she attended. Reversing the power balance within their relationship was going to take time, but they were already on the way. Claire had poured her heart out to Heather, had admitted that America had been a big mistake and that she had become involved with a married man who had damaged her emotionally, leaving her badly equipped to discover a sister who was not only going somewhere with her career but in love with a man who adored her back.

Now she rented the flat that had been Heather's, as Heather and Theo had moved to his country house—the perfect place, Theo said, grinning, in which to bring up the children they would have together.

In the silence of the bedroom, after a blissful marathon of lovemaking, Heather gazed adoringly at Theo as he slept, his ridiculously long lashes drooping against his cheekbones. His hand rested possessively across her and she sighed with pure pleasure, adjusting her body so that long brown fingers slipped across her breast and lay there. He opened his eyes and smiled at her.

'You wanton woman,' he murmured in a low, sexy voice. He marvelled at how, every time he looked at her, he felt his heart swell with pure adoration.

'Well…' she gazed at him with a smile '…we have to get a move on if we're to fill some of these bedrooms with the pitter-patter of tiny feet…'

MILLS & BOON® PUBLISH EIGHT LARGE PRINT TITLES A MONTH. THESE ARE THE EIGHT TITLES FOR NOVEMBER 2006

❦

THE SECRET BABY REVENGE
Emma Darcy

THE PRINCE'S VIRGIN WIFE
Lucy Monroe

TAKEN FOR HIS PLEASURE
Carol Marinelli

AT THE GREEK TYCOON'S BIDDING
Cathy Williams

THE HEIR'S CHOSEN BRIDE
Marion Lennox

THE MILLIONAIRE'S CINDERELLA WIFE
Lilian Darcy

THEIR UNFINISHED BUSINESS
Jackie Braun

THE TYCOON'S PROPOSAL
Leigh Michaels

MILLS & BOON®

Live the emotion

1006 Rom LP

MILLS & BOON® PUBLISH EIGHT LARGE PRINT TITLES A MONTH. THESE ARE THE EIGHT TITLES FOR DECEMBER 2006

❧

LOVE-SLAVE TO THE SHEIKH
Miranda Lee

HIS ROYAL LOVE-CHILD
Lucy Monroe

THE RANIERI BRIDE
Michelle Reid

THE ITALIAN'S BLACKMAILED MISTRESS
Jacqueline Baird

HAVING THE FRENCHMAN'S BABY
Rebecca Winters

FOUND: HIS FAMILY
Nicola Marsh

SAYING YES TO THE BOSS
Jackie Braun

COMING HOME TO THE COWBOY
Patricia Thayer

MILLS & BOON®

Live the emotion

1106 Rom LP